A

'Mala

Miss S

silly, like spilling ink into the goldfish bowl, or

getting a halfpenny stuck up my nose.

That's because in Ireland, where I come from, if someone calls you an amadan, it means they think you're a fool. But the amadans I'm writing about here are clever little fellows who use computer screens to come through into our world to tackle crime, ably assisted by the Stroke, which is their ability to paralyse people. My first book about them, called Amadans, was great fun to write, so here they are again, getting into even more trouble.

Malachy lives in a big old house in Aberdyfi, a pretty little seaside village in North Wales, with his wife Liz and   ts, Bracken and Milo. Every morni   wn to the beach, fishing for stories, an   mes home and writes them. You can   re about him and his books on his website   w.malachydoyle.co.uk

CONTENTS

1	Dirty Doings in the Dark	7
2	Oh, Crumbs!	13
3	Haranga the Not-So-Horrible	18
4	Bad News for Partho	22
5	GoSH	28
6	Here's Haranga!	37
7	Sonya, Waking	47
8	Friends Reunited	53
9	Bad News, Barry Frizzle	58
10	Hanging on by Your Fingernails	68
11	A Riot in Dizzy Belle's	77
12	Here Comes Sonya	85
13	Unwelcome Visitors	90
14	Amadans Alert!	95
15	Stuck Fast in Limbo Land	103
16	Putting the Squeeze on Steady George	108
17	A Load of Meanwhiles	119
18	Sonya's Coming Closer	126
19	The Point of No Return	130
20	The Incredible Shrinking Hulks	136
21	Hugs and Honours	145
22	Haranga in the Bath	155
23	Kidnapped	164
24	Little Boy Lost	172
25	Onwards and Upwards	179
26	Showdown	187

For Seana Lee

www.amadans.co.uk

ORCHARD BOOKS
96 Leonard Street, London EC2A 4XD
Orchard Books Australia
32/45-51 Huntley Street, Alexandria, NSW 2015
A paperback original
ISBN 1 84362 758 2
First published in Great Britain in 2005
Text © Malachy Doyle 2005
The right of Malachy Doyle to be identified as the author
of this work has been asserted by him in accordance
with the Copyright, Designs and Patents Act, 1988.
A CIP catalogue record for this book is available from the British Library.
1 3 5 7 9 10 8 6 4 2
Printed in Great Britain

Amadans Alert

MALACHY DOYLE

ORCHARD BOOKS

1
DIRTY DOINGS IN THE DARK

It's night. A large shape appears out of an alleyway. Dark glasses on and a hood pulled up tight so you can't make out his face. A quick check that there's no one about, and then he runs, on cushioned feet, towards the door to Nita's yard.

A tug on the handle, but it's locked. A muttered curse, then a flash of a torch, up and down the alley until he sees what he needs. A couple of wheelie bins, further up the lane.

Padding over, he tests them for weightiness, smelliness, squeakiness. Then he grabs hold of the lighter, fresher, less squeaky one and trundles it off, as quietly as possible. Into position next to Nita's door and up he hoicks himself, onto the lid and up again, onto the wall.

Another quick flash of the torch, to spot a safe place to land, and his cushioned trainers break his fall as he drops gently down onto the other side, as silently as a cat. (Which is why they call them cat burglars, in case you were wondering. Not because they steal cats, or sit on your lap purring, or eat Jellymeat Whiskas.)

A third flash of light around the yard – careful not to shine it at any windows – and then he sees what he's come for. It's up against the wall, gleaming proudly in the torchlight.

'Aha!' he whispers, under his breath. 'We're in business!'

And what is it that our nasty teenage sneakthief has gone to all this trouble for? I hear you asking. What's he scuttling around in the middle of the night for? What's he balancing on bins and risking breaking his neck for?

It's Nita's younger brother, Partho's, brand new top-of-the-range mountain bike, that's what. The one he got for his seventh birthday, that very day. The one the little fellow's been dreaming about for weeks. The one that's been sitting in the window of the bike shop that he's walked past on his way to and from school every day for the past three months, crying out, 'Buy me, Partho! You know we're made for each other!' The one that had made him screech with delight when his mum wheeled it into his bedroom that very morning, all tied up with balloons and streamers, and that he was just about to bounce down the stairs on till Nita grabbed hold of him.

'But it goes up mountains,' Partho pleaded. 'Surely it can go down stairs!'

The one he'd been racing up and down the street on, in his pyjamas, before breakfast, howling with happiness. Then haring round the neighbourhood all day, doing wheelies, zoomers and all sorts of tricks, drawing admiring glances from the warm-hearted, covetous scowls from the cold...

And the dirtiest of smirks from one person in particular. The anonymous teenage bike thief, who lurks all alone in the flat above the video shop, twitching the curtain and watching for any opportunity to take advantage of someone else's good fortune. Watching and waiting, looking and listening, noticing who lives where and what they've got and where they keep it, and what they wouldn't miss – and how much it's worth to the sort of people he knows who'll give you hard cash for anything and no questions asked. (Handy people to know, they are, if you're that way inclined. Which I very much hope you're not.)

'Nice one,' the hooded burglar mutters to himself, running his thieving eyes over the shiny aluminium, the twenty-four-speed fire-trigger gears, the state-of-the-art fully active suspension, the stop-dead shimano brakes. And not a cover, not a chain, not a bike lock in sight. 'What a fool,' he smirks. 'What a silly, trusting, innocent fool.' And his thoughts turn to its re-sale value. 'Mmmm,' he says, stroking it lovingly. 'This'll fetch me a hundred, no bother.'

With as little noise as possible he picks up the featherweight bike, carries it over to the door of the yard, slides back the bolt and then he's off, down the alley and away. He's much too big for it, of course, but it's the middle of the night, there's no one about (so he doesn't mind looking stupid) and all he's got to do when he gets home is to haul it up the steps to his flat round the side of the video shop, and tuck it away in his front room until his nasty flash-cash friends come calling.

But suddenly, before he's even out of the alleyway, a shape appears in the darkness ahead of him. It's small, a lot smaller than the bike thief. It, too, has a hood, pulled up tight. It's running towards him, on silent feet, and the rider, pedalling at full speed down the lane, doesn't even notice until they've nearly collided.

'Stop!' hisses the shape in the darkness, and a long thin hand, with seven bony fingers, reaches out from inside the coat and briefly touches the thief's arm. With the Touch. The Stroke. The amadan's secret weapon in the battle against crime.

But nothing happens. The sneakthief isn't paralysed. He doesn't even slow down.

'Stop, you must stop!' hisses the frantic little creature from another world, turning full circle, running alongside, and trying to grab hold with his other arm as well.

'Push off!' cries the burglar, who's hardly even noticed him. 'Must be that kid who's been parading about on it all day, out to save his precious present,' he thinks. 'Serve him right, the spoilt little brat. Serve him right, for being such a show-off, riding it all around town like he's better than everyone else.'

And with a mighty shove, and the wickedest of laughs, the teenage sneakthief flings the caped defender aside. Then, with a quick change of gear, off he zooms, out of the alley, on to the main road, through the lights and away.

And the poor defeated amadan, in a crumpled heap among the rubbish, moans quietly. 'Clear off, you,' he mutters, eyeing an arch-backed ginger cat, hissing down at him from the wall above. 'I might not have enough power to paralyse humans any more – not since that stupid big monster, Haranga, started mucking about with the Stroke – but I could freeze you to the wall for the rest of the night, no bother.'

The silent onlooker, unimpressed, of course, in the way that cats always are, turns his back and struts away, head held high. While the furious little amadan, embarrassed at having been seen to fail in his crimestopping duty yet again, picks himself up, dusts himself down, and stomps off into the night.

2
OH, CRUMBS!

'Finished on the computer already? That didn't take long.'

It was earlier in the evening, and Jimmy's father had just looked up from his newspaper, as Jimmy, Nextdoor Nita (Partho's big sister) and Jimmy's grandad entered the room.

'Yeah, thanks Dad. We've done what we needed to.'

'Great.' Jimmy's dad reached out to snaffle the tin of chocolate biscuits from the table in front of him. 'I'm just going back in to work on my book, then.'

'Oh yes, the Great Irish Novel?' said Nita, smiling. 'How's it going, Mr MacIver?'

'Mmm, all right,' replied Dad. 'I'm still on

Chapter Two, as it happens, but it's coming along.'

'What page?' asked Nita.

'Pardon?'

'What page are you on?'

'Well, eh, only page nineteen, since you asked.' Jimmy's dad was a bit sheepish. 'But it's going rather well at the moment, though I say it myself.'

'Good. That's good. How long have you been working on it, by the way?'

'Oh, well, eh…' He was getting edgy under the weight of all Nita's questions. He really wanted to escape into his writing room, but for some odd reason couldn't seem to lift the biscuit tin from the table. He looked directly at it, for the first time, only to see someone else's hand holding it down from above. A smaller hand. A Jimmy hand.

'Leaving any for us, Dad?'

'Yes, eh, right. Of course. You can have the rest, Jimmy. Share them out between you.' Giving up, he wandered off into his study.

'That was a bit mean, stopping your dad having his biscuits,' said Nita to her friend, once Mr MacIver had gone. 'They probably give him inspiration.'

'Tooth rot, more like, the amount he gets through. Anyway, it's a bit much, him telling me to share them,' answered Jimmy. 'There's never anything but crumbs, by the time I get near them. And what about you, Nita, if we're talking about meanness?'

'Me? What about me?'

'Well, if anybody's mean, it's you, having a go at him about his book like that.'

'I was only...' Nita thought about it. 'Well, maybe it did sound a bit hard. But he's been going on about his "Great Irish Novel" since the dinosaurs roamed the earth. Why doesn't he just give up on it and write another fantasy book, like that one he did before.'

She went over to the bookshelf that ran, tall and proud, all the way along the opposite wall and ran her fingers over the titles until she found the one she was looking for. 'It's great, this one,' said Nita. 'I really want to know what happens next.'

'Me too,' said Jimmy. 'But Dad's got it in his head that he's got to write something serious this time. Something he'll be remembered by when he's gone.'

'Why, where's he off to?' Nita looked up in surprise.

'No idea.' Jimmy shrugged his shoulders. 'Down to the shops to buy some more chocolate biscuits, probably.'

He opened the tin and stared deep into the darkness. Upending it, he tapped on the bottom and out dropped the last lonely biscuits – one, two and a handful of crumbs. He was just about to shove the first one in his mouth when he remembered that he'd agreed to share them, so, sighing deeply, he handed them round. One to Nita, one to Grandad, and the handful of crumbs for himself.

But Jimmy's old grandad was staring at the biscuit he'd been given like he'd never seen one before in his life. The chocolate coating slowly melted in his wrinkly paw as he looked up, at Jimmy, Nita and all the way round the room, before muttering something incoherent and stumbling off to bed.

'I think all that excitement we had with the amadans must have worn him out,' said Nita, thinking back to how Grandad had helped her and Jimmy confront the mighty monster, Haranga. 'I did tell you it'd all be too much for him,' she said, wiping the melted chocolate off the door handle (she always was a tidy, organised person, was Nita).

'No way, Nita. Grandad's not finished yet.' Jimmy was having none of it. Sure, hadn't his crazy old grandad been the star of the show ever since the amadans had called them through to help them? Sure, where would they have been without Grandad and his secret weapon – his bowl of cold, sticky porridge which he always had at the ready to launch at anyone and everyone who threatened them.

Yes, Jimmy was going to stick up for his mad old grandad, even if he had deprived him of the very last chocolate biscuit, and wasted it too. 'He's a MonsterBuster, good and proper,' he told Nita. 'Has been all his life. A decent night's sleep, a big bowl of porridge for breakfast, and he'll be fine. Just you wait and see.'

3

HARANGA
THE NOT-SO-HORRIBLE

Meanwhile, back in the palace of the Queen of the amadans, in the world beyond the computer screen, Haranga, the mighty monster, who'd been the cause of all the problems in the first place, was doing his level best to be a reformed individual. He'd apologised for trying to stop amadans having the power of the Stroke – the ability to paralyse someone simply by touching them, which the spiky creatures used for good by coming over into the human world in the depths of the night and laying their hands on each and any criminal they came across, in order to temporarily paralyse them and prevent them from carrying out their dirty deeds.

Yes, Haranga had been using his own powers to damage the Stroke, in the hope that crime would run rife, the human world would descend into chaos, and he'd be able to take over here, there and everywhere. But having encountered Jimmy, Nita and Jimmy's grandad, when they came over into the amadan world to try and help, the mighty monster had eventually seen sense and was now determined to make up for his past misdeeds: to turn over a new leaf and become an upstanding member of the amadan community.

Unfortunately, though, he was already fed up with being kept prisoner. He was an active sort of a lump, you see, more used to living the wild and woolly outdoor life than sitting in a room watching the light fade from the window and dust settle on the mantelpiece. In fact, the idea of being stuck in one room for any length of time – especially one designed for creatures the size of twiddly wee amadans – was just too much for Haranga to bear.

Two steps up and three across, two steps back and three across, over and over for hours. Returning to the window every now and again to stare out with a fierce longing at the river and woods, the hills and the sky. Then, with a moaning and groaning of longing and woe, the once-mighty creature flung himself to the floor and did two hundred press-ups and three hundred sit-ups, causing the whole of the palace to creak and to quiver.

'Got to get fit!' he moaned. 'I've got to get fit.' For even though, only a matter of weeks before, he'd lain in a heap on the floor of his cave, broken, bent and bleeding, almost to the point of being dead, defunct and deceased, now he was raring to go.

'Stop all that bashing about, you stupid great lummox!' roared Queen Alisha, flinging the door open wide. 'What are you trying to do, bring the whole of my palace crashing down around us?'

Haranga blinked. The Queen of the amadans might be only a fraction of his size but she was as fierce as a fox in a chicken house when her dander was up. 'I'm bored, Your Highness,' he said, apologetically. 'I'm just trying to get a bit of exercise.'

'Well, exercise your brain, for a change, and think of the damage you're likely to cause my house, shaking it to bits like this! You'll be allowed out of here, Haranga, when I'm well and truly convinced that you're no longer a threat to the peace and security of my people, and not a moment before. Understood?'

'Understood,' muttered Haranga, trying to make himself look as small and unintimidating as possible. 'I'll try to be good.'

'You do that!' declared the Queen. 'And do it quickly, for I'll be glad to get rid of you, to tell you the truth. At least then I'll be able to use my hall again.'

'How about if I go and help out in the computer room?' suggested Haranga, thinking that it might be nice to go and see his old friend Bunsen Bernard, the Official Gatekeeper of the SuperHighway, and see how he was getting on with controlling the pathway between the amadan and human worlds. At least it'd be a change of scene, even if it was likely to be even more cramped.

'Well…' the Queen thought about it for ages – or at least it felt like ages to a monster of little brain like Haranga – and eventually decided it was worth the risk. 'Fair enough,' she said, 'I'll get one of my guards to take you over there. But you're not to mess about with the machines. You've done enough damage already, OK?

'OK. I'll try and be good.'

'You *will* be good!'

'I will be good.'

4

BAD NEWS FOR PARTHO

'Nita! Nita!' Shake, shake. 'Wake up! It's gone!'

Nita opened her eyes, and there was her younger brother next to her bed, wide-eyed and as white as a sheet.

'What's gone?' And then she looked at the clock by the side of her bed. 'Partho, it's five in the morning!'

'I know.' The despair in his voice was unmistakable. 'I wanted to see the sunrise from the top of the hill, but I can't find my bike, not anywhere. I left it in the yard when I went to bed, and it's disappeared.'

'Your brand new bike? Don't be silly, Partho. Of course it hasn't. You must have put it in the shed.'

'No, I didn't. I know where I left it. It was right outside the kitchen door.'

'Mum or Dad must have put it away, then. Stop panicking, Partho. And stop shouting, too – you'll wake everyone up. I'll come down and help you find it.'

Nita threw on her dressing gown and hurried downstairs. But her little brother was right – there was no sign of the bike, not in the shed, not round the front, not anywhere.

Then she spotted the yard door, swinging on its hinges. 'Have you been out in the alley?' she asked him. 'Was it you who left that door open?'

'No. It was like that when I came down.'

She ran over to the door, the sinking feeling in her bones plummeting to her toes, and looked up and down the lane. 'What's Jimmy's wheelie bin doing here?' she muttered to herself. And then she put two and two together and saw, in her mind's eye, the whole thing, just as it happened. A night-time sneakthief. Up and over, nick it and out.

'It's gone, isn't it, Nita?' Partho was standing next to her, drooping with disappointment. 'Someone's stolen my beautiful bike, haven't they?'

Nita could see how desperate her little brother was to hold back the tears.

'I'm sorry, Partho.' She slipped her arm round his shoulder. 'But unless they're planning to bring it back, which I must admit is pretty unlikely, I'm afraid you're probably right.'

And, with a great gulp of sadness, her little brother wrenched himself away and rushed back into the house, slamming the door behind him so fiercely that the glass shook.

And, although Nita couldn't actually see what happened next, she knew he was racing upstairs to babble out the catastrophic news to their sleeping parents – flinging himself on their bed, pounding on it with his fists. Mum would be figuring the whole thing out ten times quicker than Dad and be reaching out for him, and poor Partho would finally break down in her arms and cry his eyes out.

'You know whose fault this is?' said an indignant Nita, when she met up with Jimmy later.

'Whose?'

'Your friend Haranga's, of course! If he hadn't messed up the power of the Stroke, the amadans would have been able to stop it happening.'

'Oh, I don't know.' Jimmy had a bit of a soft spot for the outsize outrage, after all they'd been through together. 'I mean, you can't blame poor Haranga for every single thing that goes wrong in the world. The amadans always do their best, I know, but I'm sure, even before he came on the scene, they never managed to stop more than a small percentage of badness. I mean, there just aren't enough of them to cover the whole world in one go.'

'Maybe not,' conceded Nita, 'but after what we've done for them – you, me and your grandad – they owe us, remember! So, if they've only got a limited ability to keep crime down, then surely it's round here that they'll be concentrating their efforts, as a way of thanking us. And if it wasn't for your precious Haranga, they'd at least have been able to stop Partho's bike getting stolen on its very first night, from our very own backyard.'

'He's not exactly my precious,' said Jimmy, thinking *Lord of the Rings* and realising that he'd maybe pushed the solidarity with horrendous horrors a bit far, and needed to show more sympathy to Nita and her brother if he didn't want to put their friendship in danger. 'But how about we put the word out to the amadans. Maybe, even though they weren't able to prevent the bike from being stolen, they've got some idea who might have done it. Then we can try and get it back, before—'

'Before the burglar sells it on.' Nita had an annoying habit of finishing Jimmy's sentences. 'It's not as though he's going to be riding around on it. For one, it's a kid's bike and he's hardly likely to be a kid, if he goes creeping about in the middle of the night. For two, it's not just any old bike, it's a top-of-the-range mountain bike, with twenty-four-speed fire-trigger gears, state-of-the-art fully active suspension and stop-dead shimano brakes, and if we don't track it down quick it'll be out of town before you can say "aspidistra".'

'What's that?'

'What's what?' said Nita, looking all around.

'Asti... Pasti...'

'It's a house plant, silly,' said Nita, easily tempted into lecture mode, even when it was against her better interests. 'It's got broad pointy green leaves and there's one in Dad's study – you must have seen it. They used to be very popular in Victorian times, apparently, and they're sometimes called Cast Iron Plants because they can survive just about any treatment you throw at them.'

'Like Grandad?'

'Mmmm, maybe... Look, stop trying to change the subject, Jimmy. Can we please get back to what we're supposed to be talking about?'

'Astipistras?'

'No, Partho's bike!' yelled Nita. 'The poor kid's in pieces and all you're doing is rabbiting on about stupid house plants!'

'Me?'

'Yes, you. So, what are we going to do about it?'

'Water it?' There was nothing Jimmy liked better than to wind Nita up, even in a time of crisis. 'No, sorry, like I said...' He tried to sound serious, realising that the purple look on his friend's face meant he was in danger of taking things just a tiny bit too far. 'Let's get on the Web and ask the amadans. Maybe they've got some inside information.'

5
GOSH

'Dad! Dad! Can I have a go on the computer?'

'Have you made me a cup of tea?'

'Yes. It's through here.'

'Any chocolate biscuits?'

'No, but there's a sugar cube in the bowl, if you want to munch on that.'

'OK, I'll be there in a minute.'

Dot dot dot dot, dit dit dit dit, dot dot dot, beep beep beep beep beep, hisssssssssssssssssssssssssss. Click on 'home' to find the search engine. Type in www.amadansanonymous.com. Fingers crossed.

'It's Bun!'

'Hello, Jimmy. Hello, Nita. Yes, it's Bunsen Bernard, Official Gatekeeper of the SuperHighway here.' Bun loved the importance of his official role. He even had a brand-new uniform on, with GoSH in big letters on the chest and 'by appointment to the Queen' in tiny letters underneath. Wearing it in the safety of the control room, he found himself speaking in big words and with confidence. There was hardly a trace of the old scaredy-ba he used to be. 'Good to see you again, my friends,' he said. 'What can I do for you?'

'We need help, Bun. It's Partho, my little brother...' said Nita, elbowing Jimmy out of the way to get closer to the screen. 'Someone's stolen his brand new bike and...'

'I know.'

'You know?'

'Yes. We had a report from one of our crimestoppers, just a few hours ago. He caught the thief in the act, but unfortunately wasn't able to stop him.'

'The Stroke didn't work? He couldn't paralyse him?'

'I'm afraid not.'

'So do you know who it was? Can you tell us what he looks like? Maybe he's still in the area and we can track him down.'

'Sorry,' said Bun. 'I'll have to wait till the

crimestopper calls back in. I'll try to get a description for you. Oh, by the way, there's someone here who wants a word with you.'

Bun was suddenly edged aside and a familiar face filled the entire screen. In fact, despite the grisly smile, if it hadn't been familiar, it would have been jaw-droppingly terrifying.

'Haranga! What are you doing there?'

'Jimmy, my little lifesaver!' Haranga was over the moon to see him again, for it was Jimmy's bravery – when he'd risked his life to push Haranga out of the way of the gigantic boulder, deep in the cave, the last time they'd met up – that had set the hateful horror on the road to redemption. Up till then, he'd been a bloodcurdling maniac, good for nothing but frightening the wits out of anyone he ever came across, but what Jimmy had done had made Haranga reconsider everything he'd ever stood for. Which is why he'd been stuck in the Great Hall of Queen Alisha's palace, while she tried to decide whether he was a sufficiently reformed character, safe to be allowed to walk the streets alone.

'Hello, Nita,' Haranga carried on. 'Queen Alisha was fed up with me cluttering up the Great

Hall, so she said that if I promised to be good I could help Bun out in the control room for a while.'

'As long as you keep your fat fingers off the buttons,' came Bun's voice from the side.

'OK, OK, keep your hair on, mate,' cried Haranga, over his shoulder. 'Anyway, how's things out there in humanland, my best buddies?'

'Terrible,' groaned Jimmy. And he told him all about Partho's birthday, Partho's bike, and Partho's bad, bad, day.

'It's my fault, I know it is,' moaned Haranga, once he'd taken it all in. A cloud of gloom filled his fat face.

'Not really.' Jimmy tried to console him. 'I mean, you can't expect the amadans to stop every single bit of crime, Stroke or no Stroke.'

'No, it's definitely my fault,' insisted Haranga. 'Me and my stupid plans to dominate the world. I wish I'd never even thought of them. So, I'll tell you what I'm going to do. I'm going to come round there and sort that bike thief of yours out, once and for all.'

Bun's face reappeared on the screen, squeezing in front of the hairy giant. 'I'm not sure what Queen Alisha would have to say about that. You know you're not supposed to leave the castle till she gives the go ahead, Haranga. And you're certainly not supposed to go messing about in the human world. You've caused enough trouble there already.'

'Oh no,' vowed Haranga, 'I've learned my lesson, good and proper, Mister Bun. My days of messing things up are well and truly over. I intend, from here on out, now that I've seen the light, to use my bulk and my brawn as forces for good and not for evil. And the first thing I want to do with it, now that I'm a reformed character, is to bounce that bike thief out into the limitless stratosphere. So what do you think, Jimmy, you little lifesaver, you? Do you want me to come over there and do the business?'

'Well…' Jimmy hesitated. 'I'm not sure I want you to actually bounce anyone into the stratosphere. There might be laws against things like that. But if you think you could get Partho's bike back in one piece, and maybe while you're at it, teach the guy who stole it a bit of a lesson: not to pick on little kids…'

'Yes!' cried Nita decisively, her little brother's unhappiness causing the spirit of revenge to course through her blood. She wasn't one for violence, normally, preferring to sort things out calmly and logically, but in this case she was mad. Completely over-the-top mad. 'Let's do it!'

'I'll have to have a word with the Queen,' insisted Bun. 'And then, only if she agrees, mind you, I'll have to see how we can get Haranga through the screen. It's not exactly designed for creatures your size, you know,' he said, looking the outsize outlaw up and down and frowning. 'It was hard enough getting your grandad through last time, Jimmy, never mind someone the size of a...' But he couldn't think of anyone or anything the size of Haranga, as no such creature had ever been known before in the history of the amadans, so his voice trailed off into a quizzical nothingness.

'Why, is that the only way through?' said the monster, pointing at the tiny screen. 'Isn't there a proper door or something?'

'Of course there isn't a door!' Bun huffed, affecting a superior and scientific tone. 'You're talking about the SuperHighway to Other Worlds, I'll have you know, of which I am the Official Gatekeeper. It's not like nipping down the road to the shops. It is a very complicated process, the transportation of amadans into alien lands. Only to be attempted by those hand-picked by the

Queen herself, initiated and then educated into the intricacies of the SuperHighway Transference Process.'

Nita and Jimmy looked at Bun, in surprise. So many big words! So much self-importance! Bun took their raised eyebrows as admiration, and polished his GoSH badge proudly.

But when he looked at Haranga, all he got in return was a blank look. 'So you're telling me I'm supposed to climb in there,' the monster said, pointing gloomily at the screen. 'I'd hardly fit my big toe in.'

'Tell you what,' said Nita, chirpily. 'My dad's a computer engineer, and we've got a whole garage full of old monitors, waiting to be cannibalised. Why don't we lay them all out on the lawn, like a chessboard, pointing up at the sky. That way, it'll be like we've got one gigantic screen, big enough even for somebody your size to come through, Haranga. If we can imagine it hard enough. Good idea, Bun?'

'Hmmm.' Bun wasn't too sure. 'I'll go and speak to the Queen while you lot start building the screen. I'm not sure it'll work but it's…'

'Worth a try?'

'It's worth a try.'

*

'Dad, Dad, you know all those old monitors in the garage?'

'Yes.'

'Can we take them out to the garden and lay them all side by side like a giant chessboard?

'Of course you can.'

'That's one of the things I love about my dad,' said Nita, as she, Jimmy, Partho and Grandad started lugging the first of dozens of them out onto the lawn. 'He's a firm believer in having a go. Never asks why. As long as he doesn't think you're going to blow yourself up, he just lets you get on with it.'

'No humming?'

'No humming.'

'No bribing with chocolate biscuits?'

'No chocolate biscuits.'

'No need to slap him round the head with a bowl of wet porridge?' suggested Grandad, dreamily.

'No porridge.'

'Shame,' said Grandad, absent-mindedly. Then, with a whole heap of huffing and puffing, he carefully laid his first monitor in position on the grass.

'Check,' he said, happily.

'Uncheck,' said Jimmy, laying another one next to him.

'Mate, then,' said Grandad, and he lay down on the lawn and fell asleep.

6
HERE'S HARANGA!

Dot dot dot dot, dit dit dit dit, dot dot dot, beep beep beep beep beep, hissssssssssssssssssssssssssss. Click on 'home' to find the search engine. Type in www.amadansanonymous.com.

And there was Haranga. There on the screen before them.

'Where's Bun?' asked Nita.

'He went to see Alisha,' answered the monster. 'He's not back yet.'

'He left you in charge?'

'Not exactly. He told me if I touch anything, he'll bop me on the schnozzle.'

Nita laughed. 'We've laid all the monitors on the grass. I think it's big enough for you to get through. I'll turn this screen off, so you're connected up to the giant one instead. Then have a go at climbing through, while Jimmy and Grandad and me imagine, imagine, imagine you here in our world, and we'll see what happens.'

'But what if Bun comes back? He'll go mad. And I don't really want to be bopped on the schnoz, thank you very much.'

'Do it quick, then, before he sees you.'

So she switched off the monitor and they all ran out into the garden. Well, Jimmy and Nita ran. Grandad, who they'd woken up to come and watch, only ambled. Which was quite fast enough – when you're a thousand and six, or whatever outlandishly ancient age he was, an amble is the equivalent of a hundred-metre sprint.

'Imagine, imagine, imagine,' instructed Nita, so all three of them closed their eyes as tightly as possible. Grandad promptly fell asleep again, which is what happens when you're a thousand and six and you close your eyes, but Jimmy and Nita imagined, imagined, imagined Haranga forcing his bulk into Bun's screen and trying to clamber his way down through the complicated tubes of the SuperHighway.

But he must have gone in rear end first, so his schnozzle was still pointing Bun-wards, because suddenly they heard a bop, an ouch and a squeaky voice saying, 'What do you think you're doing, you stupid lump? Get out of there! I told you not to touch anything!'

The Official Gatekeeper of the SuperHighway was back from Queen Alisha. And decidedly upset at what was going on in his absence.

'You could have waited!' Bun shrilled at them, when they reconnected up in Nita's dad's study. 'It's not very nice, being Official Gatekeeper of the SuperHighway and having your authority bypassed!'

'Sorry,' said Nita.

'Yeah, we're sorry,' echoed Jimmy.

'Duh,' said Haranga, rubbing his poor sore nose. 'It's not very nice being bopped on the schnoz, either. Especially when you're not even looking.'

'Anyway…' began Bun, reasonably happy again now he'd had an apology. He never could manage to stay cross for more than a couple of minutes, could Bun. It's part of the burden of having the sunny disposition of an amadan – even if you want to be fed up and angry, you can't for long. 'Queen Alisha's so keen to get this ugly big lump out of her hair and her hall that she's given permission for us to try out your suggestion, Nita,' he told them. 'I'm still not convinced it'll work – this whole chequerboard idea – but then it's only Haranga… I suppose there's no great loss if he disappears down the plughole of transference.'

Haranga gave him a look. A monstrous look.

'Only kidding,' said Bun, slightly nervously. 'OK, let's have a go!'

So Nita closed down the screen again, and they ran out to the garden, and imagined, imagined, imagined, as hard as they possibly could. And slowly, slowly, through the chequerboard of monitors appeared the giant nose, the face, the head, the neck, the hands, the arms, the shoulders, the chest, the body, the legs and the feet of Haranga.

'Schlooo—

ooooooo—

oooooo—

oooooo—

oooooop!'

And at last he was out and up and towering above them.

'It worked!' cried Nita. And it had, sort of. But it hadn't, sort of, too. It was Haranga, all right, but when you looked more closely you realised that the chequerboard effect meant that where there'd been a gap between screens, there were gaps in

Haranga, too. So that he actually looked like ninety percent monster and ten percent invisibility. Or like a patchwork quilt version of himself that hadn't been sewn together yet, so all the squares of material were floating about in thin air, in roughly the right relation to each other, but not quite. So that somehow he didn't seem nearly as scary as he used to, because it looked as though a decent gust of wind might blow him away. Or that the constituent parts of Haranga, with no real skeleton to hang on to, might at any moment slither downwards like melting ice and end up in a soggy, boggy heap upon the floor.

'Jimmy!' he beamed, bending down and scooping up his saviour. 'How are you doing, kid? Give me five!' At least his great booming voice hadn't changed. At least it didn't disappear into the ether through the holes in the middle.

Then he greeted Nita and Grandad, who'd been woken up by all the schlooping. Jimmy and Nita managed to withdraw their hands before Haranga's great chubby paw came crashing down on top (the perfect recipe for broken bones). And Grandad was quick-thinking enough to make sure it was his hand that did the downward smacking, loaded up with porridge – he always kept a small supply in his pocket for emergencies, just to show who's boss. (A messy business, high-fiving people with a fistful of porridge. Best not to try it at home. Not over the living-room carpet, anyway.)

And, when all the business of greetings were over, Haranga said, 'Where's that little brother of yours, Nita? Bring him here, and then let's go and get his bike back.'

Partho was up in his bedroom. He was trying to read a book, but he couldn't keep his mind on the plot for more than a few sentences at a time. His mind was full to bursting with anger, regret and sadness. All he could think of, really, was his beautiful bike. How it was the best present he'd ever had in his life and how incredibly unfair it was that he'd only had it for one day, before it was gone for ever.

How – although he was only seven years old, and there was a very good chance he'd live ten times as long and more, which gave him oodles of time for all sorts of horrible things to happen, as well as all the amazingly wonderful stuff he was planning to get up to – he didn't see how he was ever likely to have a sadder day in his whole livelong life than this one.

Nita knocked on the door. 'Can I come in?'

Partho grunted.

'How are you?' she said, edging it open.

Partho grunted again.

'Still sore about the bike?'

'What do you think?'

'Would you like us to help you try and find it?'

'We've tried. What else can we do?' Partho shrugged his shoulders as though he didn't really care any more. Which he did. But they'd already been all round the neighbourhood, looking for it. They'd asked everyone to report back if they heard or saw anything. They'd rung the police. They'd put posters up on all the lamp-posts. What more could they do? It was gone. Gone, and he might as well get used to it.

'If you come down to the garden shed,' Nita told him, 'there's something I want to show you.'

Partho's eyes lit up, all of a sudden. Which showed he hadn't quite lost all hope.

And Nita, seeing the fire in her little brother's eyes, immediately realised her mistake. 'No. I'm sorry, Partho. It's not your bike. But it's someone who might be able to help us.'

'Who is it?' There was a lifeless tone back in his voice.

'I can't tell you, I'm afraid. Not here. But it's

someone special. Someone secret. That's why he's hiding in the shed.'

Partho said nothing. But you know how it is – if somebody offers to include you in a secret, it's incredibly hard to say no, even if you can tell it's probably only going to end in disappointment. Especially when you're only just seven. So eventually, the thought of someone hiding in the shed was enough to tempt him to at least go and see. And, without a word, without making it look as though he thought there was any real point, he put down his book and followed Nita down the stairs and across the yard.

And there, in the darkened shed, sitting around on barrels and wheelbarrows – anywhere they could find a space, basically – were Jimmy, Jimmy's grandad and, to the young boy's utter amazement, Haranga – the patchwork Haranga – almost bent double to squeeze into such a small space, but horrendous-looking nevertheless.

'It's all right,' said the hideous hugeness, seeing the little boy's fear. 'I know I look a bit scary but I don't hurt people. Not any more. Not unless they deserve it.'

Partho met his eyes. 'I don't deserve it,' he whispered.

'I know,' said Haranga, smiling. 'And you don't deserve having your bike nicked, either. So I've come to see if I can help you get it back.' And he proceeded to explain about the amadans. About the Stroke, and its purpose on earth. And how, through Haranga's own pride and stupidity, its power for goodness had been diminished, so that now there was no way of stopping crime.

'When Jimmy and Nita told me about your brand new mountain bike, and how it was your pride and joy,' he said, 'I knew it was my fault you'd lost it. So I've come along to try and rescue it, and give that bike thief of yours a good scare at the same time.'

Partho's eyes lit up again, and later, much later – when everyone sensible was curled up in bed and only nightworkers and criminals were out and about – he and Nita tippy-toed back downstairs, where they were joined in the yard by Jimmy and his grandad, who was carrying his secret weapon in case things got tough: a big bowl of soggy porridge.

They opened the door of the shed and heard the most ear-deafening noise. It was the rake, shaking. The spade, rattling. The watering can, vibrating. All caused by the overpowering sound of Haranga, snoring his head off. (It wasn't a proper sleep, of course, as he only needed one of them every hundred years. Just a little doze.)

'Duh. Where am I?' he asked, coming to the surface as Jimmy shook him, hard.

'Here. In my garden shed,' whispered Nita. 'Wakey, wakey, big fellow. We're off into the night to see if we can track down Partho's bike.'

Haranga clambered out, as quietly as possible. The fresh air brought back his energy, and he looked down at the little fellow, Partho, and winked. Then he lifted him up onto his shoulders and off they went, out of Nita's yard and into the pitch-dark alleyway.

7
SONYA, WAKING

Sonya woke. And stretched. And felt the hunger in her stomach.

She was used to the hunger in her stomach. When you slept for a hundred years at a time, you always woke with sharp pangs of hunger in the pit of your stomach. But something else was wrong. Something new. Something different.

Her beady eyes darted all around, scouring the darkness. Sonya was used to darkness, too. When you lived at the back of a cave, you were accustomed to darkness. And then she realised, with a heart-rending shock, the cause of her deep feeling of unease. She was alone.

'HARANGA!' she screamed, her deep, deep voice booming off the walls of the cave. 'WHERE

ARE YOU, LITTLE BROTHER?'

Her eyes were drawn to the open doorway, where she tried to focus on something that she could just about make out, standing there. Was it Haranga, her one and only soulmate, waiting for her to wake from their sleep of a hundred years? But the blinding light, streaming through the open doorway either side of the darkness was too bright – far too bright – and she had to look away.

'Haranga!' she cried, blinking away the pain of the dazzlement. 'Is that you?' But there was no response.

Narrowing her eyes, then, until they got used to the fierceness of the light, Sonya rose up onto her creaky legs and dragged her massive bulk forward. But as she got closer to the entrance, where she could stand fully upright without bashing her head on the roof of the cave, she realised that the dark shape was nothing but the same old rock that had stood guarding the doorway for thousands of years. That was there, every time she and her brother woke. That, in her long, long, hundred-year sleep, she had forgotten about, yet again.

'Damn you, rock!' she said, punching it with her fists. 'Damn you, for pretending you're my brother. Damn you, for trying to trick me!' And she bashed and crashed at it, over and over, pummelling it with her arms, her legs and every available part of her mighty and muscle-bound body, until the poor defenceless boulder crumbled to dust at her feet.

Then, 'HARANGA!' Sonya screamed, staring out at the vast and empty landscape. 'WHERE ARE YOU, HARANGA?' And her voice roared through the treetops, bouncing up and off the snowy peaks and filling the whole of that unpopulated land with echoes of her distress.

There was no one to hear. For Haranga, her only family, her only friend, her only companion in that cold and lonely world, had left without her.

'Curse you, brother!' she shrieked, realising that he was gone and not coming back. 'Curse you, for leaving me here, alone, unloved and abandoned!'

For a horrible feeling, deep down inside, told Sonya, beyond a shadow of a doubt, that this time she *was* alone. That it was not just hunger that had sent her little brother out before her, but that he had decided, after all this time, to leave this cold and bitter land in search of a better place, to leave his one and only sister to her fate. How cruel, to desert the one and only person who had

49

looked out for him ever since that terrible day when their parents had disappeared into the darkness, never to return. How cruel of Haranga, the ungrateful wretch, to clear off and leave his poor devoted sister to stew in her own juices.

Trickles of tears melted the snow all around her, as Sonya faced up to the lonely prospect of life on her own. But, all in an instant, the anger returned.

'I shall find you, brother,' she hissed, fury filling her massive frame. 'You think you can get away from me, but YOU CANNOT! I shall track you down, wherever you are, and I shall get my revenge! Oh yes, brother, despite the fact that we share the same blood, the same history, I shall get my revenge on you for leaving me behind!'

And off she stomped, down to the frozen forest floor, to partake of the Hundred Years Hunt. But this time, it was not a hunt of celebration, as it had always been before. This time, it was not a hunt of brother and sister, stalking the land in tandem, one big and one bigger, working together to assuage the hunger of a century. This time, it was not a celebration of the fact that they had risen again from their deep and restorative slumbers, their strength, power and partnership intact.

For usually, it very soon became a feast of gluttony, a feast of overindulgence (the land having populated and repopulated in their absence, with no other predator to feed upon it), and Sonya and Haranga, those two most hideous monstrosities, could feast to their hearts' content.

But this time was different. This time, because her traitorous little brother had gone off hunting alone, everything was different. This time, despite the fact that Sonya knew there were birds and animals all around, watching her from the safety of their hiding places, it was vastly more difficult to catch them by surprise.

For Haranga had already been there before her and scared the living daylights out of any living, breathing creature he'd come across. Whatever he hadn't eaten had already been alerted by his great gallumphing footsteps and gone deep into hiding. And anything that hadn't, had been alerted by his sister's desperate roaring.

So that by the end of the first day of her return to the land of the living, there was little food in Sonya's stomach and little else but the spirit of revenge growing ever deeper in her heart.

It was time to move out of their happy hunting grounds, she decided. Time to follow her brother's footprints. For, of course, Haranga – who wasn't the cleverest joker in the pack – hadn't considered how big, fat footprints in the snow are the easiest thing in the world to follow. And those of Haranga were the biggest, fattest footprints you were ever likely to find (apart from Sonya's, of course, given that he was only her little brother and she was even bigger and fatter than him).

Sonya was the most determined, angry and cunning tracker you were ever likely to come across. So it would only be a matter of time until she caught up with him. And then he'd be sorry. Oh, yes.

8
FRIENDS REUNITED

Meanwhile, back in the real world, Haranga was making his way out into the pitch-dark alleyway, when he collided with Jimmy's wheelie bin. And sent it flying.

'Shhhhhhhhhh,' hissed Nita, as the clumsy great oaf tried to put it back in place as quietly as possible.

And they padded down the lane.

Then 'Squeeeeeaaaaakkkkk!'

'What's that?' hissed Nita. 'Who's there?'

'Squeeeeeaaaaakkkkk!' it went again, like one of those horrible scrapy noises that sets your teeth on edge.

'What's that?' hissed Jimmy. It was so dark in the alleyway that they couldn't see a thing. And

Nita hadn't brought her Sooper-Dooper High-Powered Triple-Action Drain-the-Battery-in-Five-Seconds-Flat Searchlight. (She'd thought of it, actually, but the batteries had run out from using it the night before.)

They tippy-toed to the corner. (Well, Haranga tried to tippy-toe. It's a bit like a hippopotamus trying to dance *Swan Lake*. Not a pretty sight.) Then they peered round the corner into the next alleyway, and saw a tiny crack of light where no light should have been.

'What's that?' hissed Nita, edging towards it, focusing her eyes hard to try to understand where it was coming from. And then she saw something that looked like a spider in the centre of the light. 'What is it?' she hissed, edging even closer. Brave girl, was Nita. Not afraid of spiders, strangeness, Harangas or even midnight sneakthieves. And she realised, as the crack of light inched bigger, that it wasn't a spider – that it was a spiky little hand, with seven fingers on.

'Squeeeeeaaaaakkkkk,' went the noise, and, as the light increased, every one of them could see that it was a manhole cover being lifted very slowly from below. A blinding beam of light glared out and upwards into the night, and a spiky little creature clambered out, using all of his strength to hold up the heavy metal lid for two more of the same, before dropping it down with a clank.

'Amadans!' cried Jimmy with delight, running to greet them.

'It's Jimmy!' came the high-pitched cry of the first one, running towards him, in the joy of recognition.

'And Nita!' said a female amadan, excitedly, also running towards them.

'And it's Grandad!' cried the third, a rather rougher-looking, slightly older-looking one.

'Hey, Jola!' Jimmy whooped, high-fiving him.

'And Fleur!' cried Nita.

'And my old friend Dunk!' laughed Grandad. For it was three of their favourite amadans, come to help.

'Bun thought he'd better send reinforcements,' Fleur told them. 'Just in case Haranga does something stupid.' Haranga gave her a look.

And then off they all went to do the business – to find Partho's long-lost bike and give the midnight sneakthief a good seeing-to.

Down the alley they went, across the road to the shops, down the empty high street and all the way to the video shop. Because word had spread – through the worldwide network of amadan crimestoppers – that the most likely candidate for a bike thief in their area, in fact for any sort of theft, was a Master Barry H. Frizzle, 37a Sinclair Street, Newborough (above Hollywood Videos). Aged about eighteen. Grungy teenager. Living on his own. (Having been chucked out by his parents for lying in bed all day and being nothing but trouble all night.)

He'd been stopped in the act of pinching things on countless occasions by amadans, when their power was at its peak. Stereos, car radios, bikes, handbags – you name it, he'd had it. Or tried to. And, on other occasions, once the power of the Stroke had been weakened – thanks to the misguided efforts of the previously unreformed Haranga – and they couldn't actually stop him from perpetrating his evil misdeeds, the crimestopping amadans had taken to following Barry Frizzle home, keeping an eye on what he did with his ill-gotten gains, and logging all the info through to head office, i.e. Bun.

And now, with sufficient reinforcements, it was time to go and deal with the troublesome teenager on his home turf. Time to give him a dose of his own medicine. Time for him to meet not only the horrendous Haranga and three angry amadans, but to confront Jimmy's grandad – scourge of bullies everywhere; to face Nita – all teeth, curls and anger; Jimmy – all brash boyish bravado; and Partho – small but perfectly furious at the theft of his most prized possession ever, stolen on the night of the very first day he'd got it.

9

BAD NEWS, BARRY FRIZZLE

Master Barry Frizzle's in the bath. Eating lemon meringue pie from the packet (stolen from the corner shop the night before). Which isn't exactly how you're supposed to eat this particular brand of lemon meringue pie – in fact, it isn't lemon meringue pie at all. At this stage, it's just gunk, and pretty foul-tasting gunk, for that matter – but Barry H. Frizzle never could be bothered doing things the way you're supposed to. Not at playgroup. Not at school. Not in the institution for trying to put troublesome teenagers back on the straight and narrow (he'd escaped, out of a toilet window – with a box full of petty cash from the office). So he's hardly likely to start now.

There's a clunk, clunk, clunking up the fire

escape (37a Sinclair Street is round the side of Hollywood Videos and up the steps), followed by a rap, rap, rapping on the door. And Barry Frizzle's expecting visitors, important visitors carrying cash, so he jumps out of the water, throws a towel around his middle and drips himself across the carpet to the door.

At the sight that greets him he throws up his hands in horror, the towel drops to the floor, and his visitors – who are not the visitors he was expecting, not by a long chalk – throw up their own hands in horror at the sight that greets them. Except Haranga, who's perfectly used to yuckiness. He looks past the naked sneakthief, spots Partho's bike against the back wall, and gives the surprised teenager a clout across the chops.

Then, 'Surprise, surprise!' says Jimmy, jumping on Barry Frizzle's poor naked foot.

'Judgement day!' cries Grandad, splatting him with a gobbet of goo.

'You dirty rat, you burgled my brother!' hisses Nita, whacking him on the knee with a well-aimed karate chop, while Dunk, Fleur and Jola hold him as steady as they can, using the last remaining traces of the Stroke.

And as Master Barry H. Frizzle, the pilfer king of sweet-and-sour, drops to the floor, stunned, stroked and soundlessly gasping for mercy, a delighted young Partho clambers over him, eyes fixed on his prized possession.

'My bike, my lovely bike!' he yells, hugging it tighter than a teddy bear. Who cares if he gets oil on his T-shirt? Partho doesn't.

And that would have been that. All done. Happy ending. Short sequel. Except that Master Barry Frizzle's timing was almost exactly right. His unexpected guests had caught him by surprise, yes indeed, but *they* were just about to be taken by surprise, too, by some rather more expected guests: his flash-cash friends, a couple of ne'er-do-wells named Black-Eyed Pete and Steady George, who were on their early-morning rounds, and climbing the steps to the flat at that very second.

'What have you got for us today, Barry Boy?' cries Black-Eyed Pete, so called because he's never seen without his sunglasses on, rain or shine, Spain or prison. Does he have any eyes? Nobody knows.

Hopping up the steps, two by two, confident of a satisfactory response (always a good place to start their rounds, is Barry Frizzle's – go see him before breakfast – never lets you down), Pete crashed into the outstretched stomach of the mighty Haranga.

Bouncing off him, then, goes Black-Eyed Pete, careering backwards into the also-quite-capacious-though-nothing-like-up-to-the-mark-of-a-monster stomach of his boss, Steady George, so called because he's very good with money and never EVER loses his cool. Who promptly loses his cool, for the first time in I-don't-know-how-long, and starts clouting his right-hand man round the earhole for being so stupid and stepping on his toe bone.

Until he spots what it was that made Pete fall.

'Eek!' he squeaks, from the little 'O' of his overfed mouth-hole, as Black-Eyed Pete, yelling for mercy from the both of them (for it's not much fun being batted to and fro like a much-abused ping-pong ball by one horrific enormity and a cold-blooded, empty-stomached boss-man), springs down the steps, four at a time and away. At which point Steady George gets a full-frontal view of the Nightmare from Elsewhere.

'YOU!' booms Haranga, pointing his long and scary index finger straight into the eyes of Steady George. Who freezes. As frozen as he would have been had Haranga had the power of the Stroke. Which he doesn't, of course, but what he *does* have is the power to invoke sheer cor-blimey terror into the heart of anyone who sees him for the very first time, looking for all the world like a ten-ton Monster from the Deep, out to commit major and never-to-be-forgotten nastiness on your poor defenceless body.

Which he is. For he's figured out, has Haranga, that this particular villain – Steady George – is the master behind a whole load of villainy throughout the town of Newborough and beyond, particularly the thieving of Jimmy's friend's brother's birthday bike. Which means he needs to be taught a severe lesson. A lesson that will be transmitted through the long and tentacled corridors of earthly banditry, so that everyone will eventually know – everyone with evil doings at heart – that despite the fact that the amadans are temporarily incapacitated, there's a new kid on the block. A Crimestopper Extraordinaire, who'll track you down, no matter how long it takes. Who'll find you, wherever you hide, and put the squeeze on you till every last drop of badness is squished out of you and all that's left is… Nothing.

Haranga reaches out to grab hold of Steady

George. A very firm and unforgiving hold. Fleur, Dunk and Jola scamper over and cling to the gangster's leg, in the vain hope that the Stroke still has sufficient power to hold down an outsize villain.

But George hasn't risen to the top of the ranks of the criminal fraternity for nothing. Overweight he might be, now that he has Black-Eyed Pete to do the dirty work for him and all he has to do is live off the fat of the profits. Now he has a driver to drive him, a dresser to dress him, a boiler to boil his breakfast eggs for three and a half minutes exactly, and a licker to stick the stamps on his envelopes (Black-Eyed Pete, basically). But in his time, he's been a slippery customer, has Steady George. In his time, he's been in a few decent scrapes, yes indeedy, and he knows how to cope.

Keep your cool.

A level head.

Don't panic.

Play dead.

(A useful mantra. With the advantage that it rhymes, so it's easy to remember, even in times of crisis. Clever, huh?)

But better still, scarper. When you're out-manoeuvred, out-numbered, and especially, at any sight or sound of the law. Leave the others to pick up the pieces, to gather the dosh, to mop up the blood. Just get out of there, while the going's good. Bring trouble unto others, but slip away quietly before it doubles-back unto you. Another useful motto, and one that's served him well.

And one which his sidekick, Black-Eyed Pete, has obviously picked up on, as on this occasion he's already upped and off at the earliest possible opportunity. Leaving his boss to stew in his own juices. Which is something Steady George will have to take up with his supposed protector when he catches up with him. But for now, it's time to skedaddle.

And so, with his two size twelves pressed firmly together, the chief gangster springs directly upwards, as high as he possibly can. And, using the power of positive thought, concentrating all his impressive weight into his oversized feet as he thuds back down, he hits the floor of the decidedly rickety fire escape with such a mighty clatter that the sound rings out across the early-morning city silence. Shattering the beauty sleep of a large proportion of the population. Causing a million and three starlings to rise squawking into the air, cyclists on their way to the early shift at the factory to crash, postmen to drop their sacks full of letters and newspaper delivery boys to throw themselves to the ground and cover their heads with the *Daily Gossip*.

Which – with Steady George's own weight added to the even more impressive bulk of the mighty Haranga, standing there next to him – means that, with one catastrophic creak, the rickety old rusty old never-been-painted-in-twenty-years staircase detaches itself from Barry Frizzle's first floor doorstep and crashes downwards to the path below in a jumble of jagged metal.

Scrrrrr—

rrrrrrr—

rrrrrrr—

unch!

Leaving Jimmy, Nita, Grandad, Partho, Partho's bike and a stunned Barry Frizzle (who'd been staying well out of it, on the far side of the room, glued to the television again, although he couldn't quite ignore the crash bang wallop of the disintegrating fire escape), all stranded, twelve feet in the air. (For there's no way down now, except through the ceiling of Hollywood Videos.)

And leaving the three little amadans – Fleur, Jola and Dunk – clinging to the doorstep by their fingertips. (They were bounced upwards when Steady George hit the fire escape, and just about managed to grab hold of the doorstep by their spiky little fingers, just in time to stop themselves falling back down into the mangled mess.)

Their friends help them up and watch, helpless, as Steady George, miraculously uninjured yet again, though somewhat puzzled by the encounter (who on earth was that ugly enormity? And what were those shrieking spiky things?) saunters off, with a whistle in his step, down the street and away for an early breakfast. Mission unaccomplished but never mind, there's plenty more where that came from. Many more petty pilferers to call on, once he's caught up with Black-Eyed Pete, given him a rollicking for desertion in the line of duty, and they've got some food inside them. Many more petty pilferers, who aren't quite on the scale of Master Barry Frizzle, but bad enough to be going on with, for now, anyway.

While Haranga, mangled beneath a jangle of steel, is grunting and groaning, pushing and shoving, twisting and untwisting, till eventually he's free of the remains of the fire escape, with only the minimum of puncture wounds.

Round One to Steady George.

10
HANGING ON BY YOUR FINGERNAILS

Haranga looked up, embarrassed.

Jimmy looked down, amazed.

But Nita summed up the situation and arrived at a solution in double-quick time. 'Stand below me, Haranga, and I'll drop onto your shoulders.'

So the battered bruiser backed up to the wall of the video shop, stomping hard on the remains of the crumpled metal to give himself as sure a footing as possible. Pressing his back against the wall, but leaning his head forwards so there was a safe place across his capacious shoulders for her to drop. Then, Nita sat herself down on Barry Frizzle's front doorstep, her legs dangling in mid-air, and pushed off.

'Don't move!' she yelled, plummeting

downwards. Unfortunately, at that very second, Haranga wobbled. His shifting weight caused the mangled metal to buckle and bend forward. He lost his balance as his legs began slipping out from under him and, with a mighty thwack, his head thumped back against the wall.

He managed to regain his balance as Nita came crashing down onto the top of his head – rather than his neck, where she should have landed. And she probably would have bounced off, splat onto the jagged metal if she hadn't had the wherewithal to reach out at the last minute as she slipped down the side of his body, and grab hold of his long and matted hair. Which she clung to for dear life, dangling there, level with his stomach, inches from the killer spikes.

'Owww!' yelled Haranga, as the pain of having his hair so ferociously tugged coursed through him. But he managed to keep his wits about him enough to reach out, take hold of Nita, and lift her to the ground, clear of the remains of the fire escape.

'Phew! That was close,' she said, relieved to be back on dry land. Then she looked back up at the others. 'OK, your turn, Jimmy!' she yelled. 'Don't worry. It's fine.'

Jimmy wasn't convinced. In fact, he looked a whiter shade of pale, having watched what happened.

'Hang on, young'un,' said Haranga, finding a better footing so he could reassure him. 'There, it's OK now.'

So Jimmy, taking his courage in both hands, sat on the doorstep and pushed off. This time, the monster didn't wobble at all and Jimmy landed safely on his shoulders. Haranga reached up to steady him as soon as he got there, and lifted him safely to the ground.

Then Partho appeared in Barry Frizzle's doorway. 'I'm not leaving my bike,' he said.

'Of course not,' said Nita. 'Bring it over and drop it down.'

'No way!' cried her little brother. 'I've only just got it back in one piece. I'm not about to let it go crashing down there.'

'Well, what else are you going to do? You can't just fly through the air on it,' said Nita. 'We're talking real life here, you know, not *ET*!'

'It's all right, little fellow,' said Haranga, smiling up at him, reassuringly. 'I won't drop it. I promise.'

Partho still wasn't happy, but he knew he didn't have much choice, so he went over to the other side of the room and fetched his precious bike. Then, kissing the saddle farewell, he let it go and watched as it fell through the air and landed, safely, in Haranga's waiting arms.

Followed closely by Partho himself, who was so pleased at seeing his birthday present safe that, without so much as a by-your-leave, he simply stepped out into mid-air.

'Here I come!' he yelled, and poor Haranga, who was still in the process of handing the bike to Jimmy, almost wet himself at the sight of Partho, hurtling downwards. He just managed to let go of the bike, turn, throw his arms out in front of him and catch the little fellow, inches from the mess of mangled metal.

'Your turn, Grandad,' said Jimmy, as Haranga set Partho down on the footpath, out of danger.

Luckily, Grandad hadn't noticed the near misses. But he still didn't fancy the idea. 'Certainly not,' he said, peering down. 'There's no way I'm flying through the air, not at my age.'

'Oh, go on,' said Dunk. 'There'd only be you and Barry Frizzle left, once we're down, and you don't want to be stuck up here with him.'

Grandad had a look through at the unpleasant sneakthief, lounging on the sofa like a pig in swill.

(He wasn't the sort to worry about things, was Barry Frizzle. Not until he really truly had to.) 'No. You're right,' said the old fellow, having second thoughts, and realising he *didn't* want to be stuck up there with the grungy teenager. 'I don't suppose I do.'

'Come on, then,' said Jimmy. 'Be brave.'

So the old fellow – who didn't much like the idea of sitting on the doorstep and pushing off into outer space like the others had done – climbed out backwards instead, on his hands and creaky knees, and carefully, carefully, lowered himself down till he was hanging on by nothing but his fingernails.

'Let go!'

'I can't!'

'Let go!'

'I can't!'

'Climb back up then!'

'I can't!'

'Well, let go, then!'

'I can't!'

Until Barry Frizzle, who was getting fed up with all this yelling – he was trying to watch television, for goodness sake, till someone got round to rescuing him – stood up from his sofa, marched over to Grandad, got down on his hands and knees till their faces were almost level, and barked, with a maniacal grin, 'If you don't let go, old man, I'm going to bounce up and down on your fingers!'

At which point, Grandad had little choice. He detached his last remaining digits and fell, perfectly safely, into Haranga's waiting arms.

Followed by Dunk, Fleur and Jola, who'd all been sitting patiently, waiting their turn, but who had taken such a strong dislike to the unpleasant teenager that they didn't want to stay up there in his company for a second longer.

'OK, my turn now,' cried the teenage sneakthief, smiling, once all the others were safely down. He'd seen Haranga catch Grandad safely, so even though he didn't much like the idea of being hugged by the horror who'd whacked him in the chops, there didn't seem to be much alternative. 'Hold out your arms, big fellow,' he roared. 'And make sure you catch me!'

And everyone down below sniggered.

'Ha, ha,' said Barry. 'Good joke. Now, open your arms, you fat lump. I'm coming down.'

And everyone laughed out loud.

'I don't know what's so funny,' said Barry Frizzle,

grumpily. 'You've all had a go, and now it's my turn. So come on, I've waited long enough. I can hardly stay up here now you've wrecked my steps, so get me down from here, you great gallumphing monument.' He didn't seem to realise it was Steady George who'd wrecked his steps, not Haranga, but there wasn't much point explaining.

And everyone turned their backs on him.

'Hey!' cried the grungy teenager, realising at last that he was about to be abandoned to his fate. (He was a bit slow on the uptake at the best of times. And this was not the best of times.) 'You can't just leave me here, guys! I mean, what would you want to do that for. I mean, what have I ever done to you? I mean, you can't just LEAVE me here!'

But he was wrong.

They could.

And they did.

They walked (except for Partho, who cycled, of course) up the road, past the shops, down the alley and all the way back to Nita's house. From where an anonymous phone call was made to the police to say that if they wanted to find a flat full of stolen goods – complete with culprit – then they were to go to 37a Sinclair Street (above

Hollywood Videos) and ask for a Master Barry Frizzle.

'Oh, and one thing... don't forget to take a ladder with you. And a JCB, to clear away the remains of mangled fire escape. And a recycling box, for all the empty beer cans...'

'So that's Barry Frizzle out of commission for a while,' said Jimmy. They were all sitting round in Nita's dad's shed, after breakfast.

'Yeah, but it's the big man I'm after,' said Haranga, scowling. 'That Steady George character. For one thing, he got away. For two, he made a fool of me. For three,' he said, counting them off on his fingers, 'I shall not rest... I shall not rest...until I get my revenge!'

'OK, OK, keep your hair on,' said Nita, trying to quieten him down. 'I know you're fed up, but we don't want the whole world to know you're in here, now, do we?'

'No. I don't suppose we do.'

'Right then, sit quiet and we'll think of something.'

So they sat. And they thought.

And they sat. And they thought.

And then, 'Got it!' cried Jimmy.

75

'Got what?' said Nita.

'Chicken pox,' said Jimmy, grinning. 'I got it when I was six.'

Everyone huffed.

So they sat. And they thought.

And they sat. And they thought.

And then, 'Got it!' cried Partho.

'Got what?' said Nita.

'Measles,' said Partho, laughing. 'When I was four.'

Everyone puffed.

So they sat. And they thought.

And they sat. And they thought.

And then, 'I've got it!' cried Grandad.

'Brain decay?' said Nita, smiling at him.

Grandad gave her a dirty look. 'No. I've figured out how to get that Steady George character.'

'How?'

'Through his stomach.'

'His stomach?'

'Yes. You could tell, just by looking at him, that he's a foodaholic. And you could tell, by the mood he was in, that he hadn't had his breakfast yet. So let's go round the cafés and see if we can find him.'

11
A RIOT IN DIZZY BELLE'S

They tried Elizabeth's, but it was way too classy.

They tried the Milk Bar, but it was way too milky.

They tried Billy Whisper's, but it was all boarded up and there was a sign saying it'd been shut down by Health and Safety.

And then they got to Dizzy Belle's, and there, in the window, was none other than Black-Eyed Pete. Tucking into his bacon and egg, baked beans and sausage, fried bread, hash brown and ketchup. And too dim to even hide.

'Hey, Pete,' said Jimmy, pushing through the open doorway. 'Where's the boss?'

A look of horror crossed Black-Eyed Pete's face when he saw who it was. Exactly the person

Steady George had told him to keep hidden from. Exactly the last person he wanted to have catching him with a faceful of grease.

Grabbing a sausage from his plate, Pete pointed it at Jimmy, right between the eyes. But Jimmy wasn't stupid – he knew the difference between a lump of pig gristle and a Colt 45, all right, and didn't even duck. Pete threw it at him, instead, hoping to create a diversion. But all he created was a second breakfast for Jimmy, who caught the sausage between his teeth as Pete threw his chair over and ran through to the back room where Steady George – who was a fast eater and had already finished his breakfast – was aiming to do business with Dizzy Belle.

'Where's the money?' demanded Steady George. (We're going back in time a bit here. Just a few minutes.)

'I haven't got any,' replied Dizzy Belle. 'You're my first customer.'

'I'm not a customer!' said Steady George. 'I'm a gangster. And I want my cut of the takings. My five percent, like I told you before.'

'What for?'

'What do you mean, "what for"? Protection, that's what for!'

'What from?'

'What do you mean, "what from"? Gangsters, that's what from.'

'But the only gangsters round here are you and Black-Eyed Pete.'

'Exactly!' cried Steady George. 'You pay up, or we cause you major grief.'

'Look, George,' said Belle, trying to reason with him. 'You're bad for business. Since you started coming round – you and your big-noise buddy – all the regulars have started going to Billy Whisper's for a bit of peace and quiet. You make people nervous, see. You put them off their food.'

Steady George humphed.

'And not only that,' continued Belle, 'but you come in here expecting to eat and not pay for it. Is that fair? How is that fair? I feed you for nothing, both of you – bacon and egg, baked beans and sausage, fried bread, hash brown and ketchup – without a penny in return. And then, instead of you paying me, you have the cheek to demand that I pay you. I mean, what do you think I am, George, some sort of charity? Some sort of Oxfam for fat hungry gangsters?'

'Billy Whisper's, you say?' Steady George wasn't even listening. Not properly.

'That's right,' said Belle. 'And things have got to be really bad if I'm losing trade to him. For one thing, he can't cook half as well as me. I mean, have you ever eaten in there? It's disgusting, and I don't just mean the food. Everyone knows he's got a kitchen full of rats and a toilet full of cockroaches.'

'Well, you needn't worry about Billy Whisper's, Dizzy. He was closed down this very morning.'

'Closed down?' Belle was shocked. She was fond of Billy, in a funny sort of way, even if she was in competition with him. It was a tough business, running a café, especially this end of Newborough, and somehow they'd both managed to survive, so far. 'How come? What happened?'

'I put a little quiet word out to Health and Safety. Because you're right, Diz. Everyone knows about the rats and the roaches. Everyone except the council. So they rolled up at nine o'clock this morning, all pens and clipboards blazing. Told him he'd a month to put things right or he'd lose his licence.'

'So he's shut up shop?'

'I'm afraid so.'

'But why, George?' asked Belle, horrified. 'Why did you blow the whistle on him?'

80

'Why do you think, Dizzy? He refused to do business with me, and he paid the price.'

Belle was disgusted. 'Well, it won't work on me. They won't find any muck in my kitchen! I run the tidiest café in town.'

'Oh, there's ways and means, Dizzy, love,' said Steady George, with an evil sneer. 'Ways and means.'

'Look, George,' she said, trying to stay reasonable. 'What I'm trying to say is, there aren't any takings. The only breakfast I've served today is yours and Black-Eyed Pete's, and I didn't get a penny for either. So five percent of nothing is nothing.'

'Are you refusing to pay?' George was getting the message at last. He'd underestimated Dizzy's grit and determination.

'Yes, George. I haven't slaved over a hot stove for fifteen years just to give a large slice of the profits to some bully who comes in here demanding protection money.'

'And that's it? End of story?'

'Yes, George. End of story. For one thing, I can't pay you, and for another, I wouldn't, even if I could. Now buzz off and leave me alone. I've a business to run. Buzz off, or I'll put a call in to the police, just like you did to Health and Safety. I'm sure they'd be fascinated to hear what you and your stupid sidekick are getting up to these days.'

Steady George was turning puce by now. It was time to call up his partner. 'Pete! Get through here!' he yelled.

At which point, into the back room rushed Black-Eyed Pete, closely followed by Jimmy, Nita, Partho, Grandad, Haranga, Jola, Fleur and Dunk.

'It's them, Boss!' yelled Pete. 'The ugly one, the ancient one and that bunch of weirdo midgets we were up against earlier! We're outnumbered!'

'I'll speak to you later,' hissed Steady George to Dizzy Belle, preparing to run. 'I've got friends in high places. I can get you closed down, just like I did Billy Whisper's.'

'And I can get *you* locked up, you big bully!' cried Grandad, overhearing him, immediately sizing up the situation, and pulling a bowl of soggy porridge out from under his overcoat and flinging it at the self-styled gangster with all his might.

'And I can get you mashed potatoed!' roared Jimmy, picking up one of Dizzy Belle's spuds and tossing it at George's head.

'I can get you tomato sauced!' yelled Partho,

squeezing a tube of the aforementioned down Black-Eyed Pete's neck.

'And I can get you baked-beaned!' cried Nita, emptying a pan of them over Pete's head.

'I can get you salt and vinegarred!' laughed Haranga, pouring both into their hair, for good measure.

'And I can get you bangers and mashed!' squeaked Fleur.

'I can get you omelette and chipped!' shrilled Jola.

'And I can get you ham and egged!' screamed Dunk.

The amadans hadn't a clue what everyone else was on about, as such delicacies had never made it to their land, but they could read them off the menu, and they didn't want to miss out on the fun.

'And I can get you streaky baconed!' shrieked Grandad, wrapping a piece around Black-Eyed Pete's eyes, in place of his sunglasses, which had fallen off in the melée.

Dizzy Belle, confused and amused in equal measure, collapsed in heaps of laughter, while 'Help! They're all mad!' cried Pete, running blindly from the café, unable to see for bacon, beans and brightness.

But Steady George didn't panic so easily. 'I'll get you for this, every one of you,' he snarled, trying to maintain his dignity despite looking like a train wreck. 'You needn't think this is the last you've heard of Steady George, not by a long chalk.'

12

HERE COMES SONYA

Tracking, tracking, through the snow,
Tracking, tracking, here we go,
Always tracking,
Always tracking,
Always bloomin' tracking!

Sonya was fed up. She'd been clambering through the snow, following Haranga's footprints, for weeks.

Because there was one thing on her mind and one thing only. To grab hold of that great ugly brother of hers and to squeeze the living daylights out of him. Then he'd learn! Then he'd find out who was the boss round here!

But I'm sure you can understand the way

Haranga felt. Because you know what it's like when you've been bossed about for too long. There comes a point when you say to yourself, 'That's it! I've had enough.' There comes a point where you wake up one morning, see the sunlight streaming through the window, and you say, 'I'm outta here.' And that's what had happened to Haranga.

The very first light of spring at the end of the hundred years of sleep (they were the deepest of sleepers, were Sonya and her brother), on the very first morning without a howling wind, had penetrated through to the back of the cave. It had woken him up and he'd yawned and stretched and looked at his screechy big, bossy big, telly-offy big sister, fast asleep beside him, and, rather than nudging her awake, like he usually did, he'd thought, 'Time to go, big boy. Time to break free from that great ugly lump beside you, holding you down, telling you what to do, what not to do. Time to go out there into the big wide world and do your own thing, for once.'

So he'd got to his feet, as gently as he could so as not to wake her, and then, as delicately as possible, he'd tippy-toed to the mouth of the cave and out into the light. The whole of the world, as far as the eye could see, was covered with snow, but the wind had dropped away to nothing at last, and there was a whisper of spring in the air. Spring! A time of change! A time of new beginnings! A time to throw off the shackles of the past and step forward into a new year, a new life!

So, with a surge of joy, excitement and freedom in his heart, off Haranga went. A quick Hundred Years Hunt, to settle the rumblings of a stomach that hadn't been fed for a century, and then off and away. Through the forest and over the mountains. Through the snow and up to the next lot of mountains. Way beyond anywhere he had ever been before, walking, ever walking. For days and weeks, until he felt sure his left-behind sister would never find him.

Trudging ever onward, through the rain and snow, until he'd come to the edge of the land of the amadans, where he'd seen traces of other living creatures and decided that it was about time to show whoever it was that he was the boss, for once.

Yes, he'd decided, there and then, to put on a show of being the nastiest, ugliest, horriblest monster the world had ever seen, and to dominate anyone and anything he came across. Which eventually meant – once Haranga had worked out how the land lay – that he was out to become the boss of the previously disaffected young NetherWorlders, like Jola and the gang. And then to become the boss of all the NetherWorlders, like Fleur and the others. Then to become the boss of all the amadans, like Bun and Dunk and even Queen Alisha. And then, by use of the SuperHighway, to become the leader of the whole human race: that's Jimmy and Nita and Grandad and you and even me!

That'll show her, thought Haranga. That'll show that great big bossy sister of mine who's in charge round here.

And it nearly worked, of course. It nearly worked, all those amazingly ambitious plans for world domination. Till all his efforts to be the biggest, baddest creature the universe had ever seen were undone at a stroke, when young Jimmy went and showed him some human kindness when they'd first met, deep in the cave when the mighty boulder-the-size-of-a-house was about to splatter the great rampaging ruffian's brains out.

Yes, by his courage and his kindness, young Jimmy went and melted all Haranga's anger, and made him see, there and then, that it was a whole lot more fun being nice to people than being horrid. That all that happened, if you were a great big lump of a bully, was that everyone feared you, everyone hated you, everyone went out of their way to avoid you, and you were left to stew in your own resentful juices.

And now it's Sonya, Haranga's big abandoned sister, who's the one with a heart full of bitterness. Now it's Sonya who's out to get her revenge, and look out anyone or anything that gets in her way!

13
UNWELCOME VISITORS

That night, when everyone was sleeping (or dozing, in the case of Haranga), Steady George and Black-Eyed Pete tracked down Barry Frizzle (the police had let him out on bail), got him to explain where Jimmy and Nita lived, and then went round there to exact their revenge.

'Nobody streaky bacons me and gets away with it,' muttered Pete, on the way over. He'd managed to find a new pair of shades, so he felt in control again, but he wasn't a happy man. Not happy at all.

And neither was Steady George. 'I shall track that lot down, every one of them – including that fat monster and those ugly little garden gnomes – and they'll regret they ever met me. Oh yes.'

They were even less happy by the time they found the place. They'd forgotten to bring a torch, so they couldn't see a thing, and having struggled to climb over Nita's back wall (Steady George wasn't quite as young as Barry Frizzle, or quite as nimble), and stumbled round to the front of the house, looking for the best way in, Black-Eyed Pete tripped on the edge of the lawn, thumped into his boss and threw him flat-on-his-face forward, onto the grass.

Which was still full of computer monitors. (Nita and Jimmy hadn't had time to tidy them away, and Nita's dad thought that, even though they did make the place look rather untidy, it was probably some sort of art project his beloved daughter was doing, or some type of Important Learning Experience, and it wasn't for him to spoil it. He left them there. At least until tomorrow.)

So, Steady George, closely followed by Black-Eyed Pete, pitched forward onto the chequerboard of computers and, with a mighty and deeply uncomfortable crash, hit the screens.

'What was that?' cried Nita, jumping out of bed and running over to the window. She knew from the sound – a mix of crunch, eek! and whoosh – that it was probably something to do with the monitors, so she thought she'd better go and investigate. Perhaps it was some more of her amadan friends, coming to help bring the gangsters to justice. And having a spot of bother getting through.

It was too dark to see clearly, so she grabbed her Sooper-Dooper High-Powered Triple-Action Drain-the-Battery-in-Five-Seconds-Flat Searchlight from her bedside cabinet (she'd put new batteries in) and padded downstairs, out into the garden. But there was nothing to be seen. Nothing but a slightly untidy arrangement of monitors.

'That's strange,' muttered Nita to herself. 'I'm sure I heard something.'

But, despite checking the whole garden – front, back and shed – there was nothing astray, so she went back to bed. (She even had a quick look out in the alley, but didn't notice anything wrong. Jimmy's bin was still outside her gate, but that didn't surprise her. They were such an untidy lot, that family, they probably wouldn't notice it was missing for a week.) She lay there for a while, listening out for any more noise, but heard nothing. So, eventually, she fell asleep, exhausted by the escapade of the previous night.

And what had become of Steady George and Black-Eyed Pete? I hear you ask. Well, I'll tell you, in case you haven't already guessed. They'd fallen through the screens, into the world of the amadans.

You see, Bun, the Official Gatekeeper of the SuperHighway, had handed over to one of his assistants for the night. The new assistant wasn't used to working at night, hadn't had enough sleep the day before, and consequently was dozing on the job. He'd managed to stay awake long enough to deal with the usual night-time comings and goings, but unfortunately, the last time he opened up the SuperHighway to let an amadan through, he fell asleep without closing it down properly.

Which meant that because the power of the process coming upwards from earth was vastly increased by there being a super-sized screen in Nita's garden, there was nothing to stop anyone who stepped onto the chequerboard of monitors from shooting straight through into the world of the amadans. And that's what happened. Steady George and Black-Eyed Pete fell crash, bang, wallop, onto the screens, there was an almighty whoosh, and suddenly there they were, in amadan land!

Where nobody wanted them. Where they most certainly didn't want to be. And which was to cause ALL SORTS of problems.

14
AMADANS ALERT!

'Amadans alert! Amadans alert! Strangers in our midst! Strangers in our midst!'

The sirens started blaring, all round the castle.

'Get the heck off me!' hissed Steady George, pushing his sidekick away and scrambling to his feet. 'Give me space, man!' He was fed up with that fool, always shoving up next to him, crowding him out one minute, trying to hide in his shadow the next. 'You're supposed to protect me, not attack me, you twit!'

'Yeah, but where the heck are we, Boss?' said Pete, looking around. It was still dark, but it definitely wasn't Nita's back garden.

'And what the heck happened?' asked George, rubbing his head, then his knees and then his elbows. All of which had come into contact with the monitors, at high speed, and some of which were developing nasty-looking bruises.

'Yeah, and what's that infernal noise?' asked Pete, covering his ears to block out the sound of the sirens. Sensitive soul, was Black-Eyed Pete. Sensitive to bright lights and loud noises, anyway. Which is why he had to wear sunglasses, to keep out the brightness. And why he liked everything to be nice and quiet, so it didn't assail his poor eardrums.

'Some sort of alarm, by the sound of it.' Steady George's instinct to scarper while the going was good – an automatic response to any sort of siren – was already taking precedence over his instinct to feel sorry for himself. 'Let's get out of here, quick!'

So they upped and they ran into the darkest corner of the yard, just as a whole cohort of amadans appeared.

'Where are they?' cried Eric.

'Who are they?' asked Queen Alisha.

'*Are* they?' said Bun, meaning he wasn't totally convinced there was anyone there at all. 'And if they are, how did they get here?'

'What's happening?' cried all the other

amadans, running around in circles in their nightshirts and crashing into each other as they searched for intruders. 'Why's the alarm gone off?'

'Oh, for goodness sake, you lot, get ORGANISED!' yelled the Queen. 'Turn on the floodlights, someone! Turn off the sirens, someone else! Investigate every nook and cranny, everyone!'

But by the time they'd got themselves sorted into sensible search parties – which isn't an easy business when you're a bunch of half-awake amadans dragged from your beauty sleep by the most horrendous screeching – Pete and George were nowhere to be found. Because lucky for them, they'd run to exactly the right spot. The one nook and cranny in the palace that was safe from discovery.

For what nobody knew – no living amadan, that is – was that there was a secret underground tunnel running the whole length of the palace grounds and beyond, the entrance to which was right there, under a pile of weeds, in the corner of the courtyard.

George prised open the cover. He and Pete squeezed through and they pulled the lid down tight (luckily, it was fitted out with air holes you could just about see through), and waited out the search. Not very comfortably, mind you, as it was only an amadan-sized hole, and they were both, particularly Steady George, considerably bigger than that. And, as we just heard, the big bossman was already more than fed up with Pete squishing up next to him all the time.

'It must have been a false alarm,' said Queen Alisha, after a thorough check of the whole castle. 'But just in case it's not, Bun, you'd better go and see if anyone's come through the SuperHighway.'

'They couldn't have, Ma'am. It's not possible. Not without my authority.'

'Don't argue, there's a good Bun,' said the Queen, with a distinct edge in her voice. 'Just go and check.' She didn't like being woken up in the middle of the night for no good reason. And she *particularly* didn't like people arguing with her.

'Yes, Ma'am. Right away, Ma'am.'

So Bun went off to see his dozy assistant. Who had been rudely awakened by the alarm, but had seen nothing whatsoever of the Transference Process.

'No. Nothing strange, sir,' he told him. 'No, wide awake the whole time, sir. Yes, completely in control, sir. Yes, I'll let you know straight away if there's anything to report.'

And Bun, stupidly, took his word for it and didn't think to check the records, to see if anyone had come through. Which wouldn't have done any good anyway, as they'd come through the chequerboard, instead.

So everyone went back to bed, the silence and darkness returned, and Steady George and Black-Eyed Pete crept out of their hiding place.

'Crikey, more of those weirdo midgets!' whispered Pete. 'Where are we? Is this some sort of circus?'

'No idea,' said George, in a distinctly grumpy mood after being cramped into a tiny hole, never mind the fact that he was covered in painful bruises. 'But I don't like it. I don't like it at all.'

All they'd been able to make out through the tiny air-holes were a bunch of squeaky voices and a load of flitting-about-at-high-speed.

'It's sure as heck not Newborough,' said George, 'but we're here now, so I suppose we'd better make the most of it.' Steady George wasn't the sort of guy to put down roots. If the going got hot, he moved on. So here he was, moved on. Fair enough – he'd scout around, turn the situation to his advantage, and move on again. 'Let's go find some food,' he said to his sidekick. 'I don't know what folks eat round here, but I'm starving.'

Some time later, they found themselves in the kitchens of the palace – George had an unerring nose for edibles. They were pretty disgusted with the meagre rations they found, mind you – it turned out amadans were vegetarian, which George and Pete most definitely weren't.

They didn't want to run the risk of cooking anything in case the noise and smell attracted attention – better to stay anonymous, for now at least – so they were reduced to munching raw carrots, nibbling lettuce, and stuffing their faces with cold potatoes and hard-boiled eggs. Followed by fruit, fruit and more fruit.

'Yuck,' said George, to his even more appalled friend. 'If we're stuck here for any length of time, Pete, we're going to have to find some four-legged friends to eat, even if we have to kill them ourselves. Otherwise all this healthy food,' he said, with a grimace, 'is going to be the death of me.'

'Hey, Boss,' said Pete, eventually, as the early-morning sun streamed through the narrow windows.

'What?' said George, his mouth full of radish. I told you he was desperate.

'There's something funny about you,' said Pete, pointing. 'Like there's all lines down you. Oh, and across you,' he added, looking more closely. 'Like you've been taken apart and put back together, only not very well.'

'Hmmm.' George returned the look. 'Like I've been unzipped into squares and laid out side by side?'

'Yeah,' said Pete. 'How did you know?'

'Because that's just how you look,' said his boss. 'I thought it was some sort of trick of the light, or the lack of it, but it's not, is it? It's real. And it's both of us. We look like Scrabble boards.'

'Like what?' Pete wasn't the word game type.

'Like crossword puzzles.'

'Huh?'

'Like chessboards, then.' But Black-Eyed Pete was still looking dim. Hardly the sort for intellectual challenges, then. 'Draughts. Chequers. Oh, never mind, we're covered in lines. Now shut it, will you?' All that rabbit food obviously hadn't done much for Steady George's patience.

'Me, shut it? It's you that's going on about

101

stupid games I've never even heard of!'

'Me, is it?'

'Yes, you!'

And they were all for squaring up and bashing the living daylights out of one another, when they heard the sound of someone just outside the door.

They dashed into a cold room and watched through the metal grille as Bun came in for an early morning snack before he went on duty in the control room.

15

STUCK FAST IN LIMBO LAND

Steady George and Black-Eyed Pete hung about, behind the door, and when Bun came out they followed him. Then, when he went into the control room, they slipped in behind him and hid round the back of the open door.

'I'll take over now,' Bun told the dozy amadan who'd been on the night shift, and then he went over to the desk and tried to calm himself down.

The trainee left, luckily without attempting to close the door, and Pete and George watched, as quietly as possible (despite the fact that they were uncomfortably squashed up in a narrow space together, yet again), while Bun slowed down his breathing and then, as calmly as possible, began to go through the morning's work: contacting the amadans who were out on crimestopper duty, filing their reports, opening up the SuperHighway to bring home the ones who were due to return, sending out replacements, that sort of thing.

'Pull this, press this, push, push, push...' Bun had a habit of talking to himself while he went about his work, of describing what he was doing in a little singsong voice. Which made it much easier to follow, if you were a quick-on-the-uptake villain with your head poking out from behind the door, watching his every move. Especially when Bun got into conversation with one of the amadans.

'How's the Stroke?' George heard him ask someone. Someone who wasn't there.

'Hopeless,' came the reply, over the airwaves. 'You touch them, and they act as though nothing happened.'

'The Stroke?' hissed George to Pete, under his breath. 'What's the Stroke?'

'So it's not getting any better, then?' asked Bun. 'You can't stop the thieving?'

'It's useless,' came the squeaky voice of an amadan, from the other side. 'The criminals are winning. I don't know what more we can do.'

George looked at Pete, and a light shone in his

brain. 'So THAT'S why our little band of criminals so often end up empty-handed!' he muttered. 'We've been caught in the act by a bunch of do-gooding fairies!'

'Huh?' whispered Pete.

'The Stroke!' whispered George. 'They've got some sort of power to stop us thieving, the wretches! But it's good news, Pete. They're losing it. Somehow they're losing it. And if I get my way,' he said, scowling, 'I'll get rid of the interfering little baggages altogether!'

He watched and listened even more closely from then on, and by the time Bun went to lunch (leaving the room briefly unmanned, the silly fellow), George knew just about everything he needed to know about the workings of the SuperHighway.

'Lock the door, Pete!' he cried, rubbing his hands together in excitement. And then he squeezed into Bun's chair ('Blimey, why do they make everything so small round here?'), pulled a few levers, pressed a few buttons, and somehow managed to override all the security mechanisms and open up the transference channels.

Then, putting on his best high-pitched squeaky voice, he put out a general alert to call back in all of the amadans who were still out on crimestopper duties.

'Alert! Alert!' he shrilled. 'Emergency! Emergency! Everyone home! Everyone home!'

And the amadans dropped what they were doing – right there and then, all over the human world – obeying immediately, exactly as they were trained to do. Every amadan who was out on crime patrol, including Dunk, Fleur and Jola, upped and left, just like that. With no goodbyes to whoever they were with, no finishing off whatever they were up to. Just up and off and vanished in a flash, home to see what it was Queen Alisha wanted them so urgently for. (For an amadan's first priority was always the defence of his homeland. Crimestopping was an extra role they took on, when things were going well and they had people left over. But if they were ever under threat back home, everyone understood that the essential thing was to get back straight away and deal with it.)

Only it turned out that Queen Alisha didn't want them at all. And Bun didn't want them either. The only person who wanted them was Steady George, and what he wanted was to teach them a lesson they'd never forget. What he wanted, in fact, was to get all the earth-based amadans right out of the picture, in order to give himself and his merry band of no-gooders a clear hand to get on with their nasty and nefarious activities, unhindered.

So what he did – rather than let the crimestopper squad back through into the amadan world – was to cast them out into some sort of a limbo land. For Steady George – who was a bit of a dab hand at computers, as it turned out – managed to work out, in about two minutes flat, not only how to work the SuperHighway transference activity, but a fiendishly clever way to shut down the recall process before it was complete.

So that Dunk, Fleur, Jola and all the other amadans out there were sucked from the human world but left stranded in a never-never limbo land of in-between-ness. Neither here nor there nor anywhere.

16
PUTTING THE SQUEEZE ON STEADY GEORGE

'Hah! It worked!' cried George gleefully, once he'd checked on their whereabouts and verified that they didn't show up on any of the screens – that they had, in effect, disappeared from all known reckoning. 'That's sorted out those stupid gnomes and that blunderbuss of a monster, once and for all! That'll teach them not to mess about in things that don't concern them, won't it, Pete?'

'Yes, Boss. It will, Boss.' Black-Eyed Pete hadn't quite worked out what was going on, actually, but it was nice to see his boss in a good mood, so he thought he might as well agree.

'Yes, Pete. It will, Pete. And it's no more than they deserve. I'm just about fed up with them, trying to cramp my style.'

For Steady George (as we saw) had worked out, by watching and listening to Bun going about his business, what the amadans had been up to over the years. How they'd been doing their level best to damage his business interests. And how he'd be much better off without them.

But he was wrong about Haranga. He might have sorted out the amadans, but what he didn't realise was that their monster of a friend had, in fact, made his way to earth through the chequerboard, just like he and Black-Eyed Pete had, and not by the SuperHighway, like everyone else. And even if he had realised it, he would have had major problems doing anything about it. For controlling the chequerboard was a whole different ball game, a whole new kettle of fish, and one which even Bun (O GoSH) hadn't quite mastered yet, in the short time it had been around.

Not that Steady George had ever realised, before, what they'd been up to, of course, because encounters between amadans and do-badders are always forgotten. But now that he finally knew what they'd been doing, he could understand why so many of his planned escapades had come to nothing. And now that he'd put the kybosh on them, he'd be able to do whatever he liked in future. No bother.

'Right, Pete!' he said. 'There's no point hanging about here. Let's get back to town and find something decent to eat.'

'Dizzy's?' suggested Black-Eyed Pete, salivating at the very thought of her bacon and egg, baked beans and sausage, fried bread, hash brown and ketchup. Just what you need after a diet of rabbit food.

'Maybe,' said George. 'We'll see if she's come to her senses yet. And then, once we've tanked up on a load of grease, I think it's time we got on with a bit of badness, now that I've stopped those annoying little amadans from cramping our style.'

But when he opened the line up again, to send himself and Pete back home, through the SuperHighway this time (but without freeing up the trapped amadans, of course – he wanted them to stay in there for as long as possible and preferably for ever), guess who was waiting for them on the other side? One very angry Haranga!

'What have you done to my friends?' roared the monster. For there he was, right there in front of them, in Jimmy and Nita's alleyway.

He knew something was up, did Haranga, for

one minute Dunk and the other two amadans had been with him in Nita's shed, having a bit of a chinwag, and the next minute they were gone, kaput, vanished into thin air. No goodbyes. Nothing.

'What friends?' Steady George tried to look innocent. And failed completely. Which wasn't surprising, since innocence and Steady George didn't exactly go hand-in-hand. He hadn't, in fact, looked even the slightest bit innocent since he was toddling about in a nappy, and even then it was only a front – as soon as his darling mother's back was turned he'd be pinching the feeding bottle from the poor kid in the next pushchair, sucking it dry and then bashing him over the head with it. So he wasn't likely to start now.

'My friends, the amadans!' yelled Haranga.

'What amadans?'

'You're lying!'

'How can I be lying?' cried the gangster. 'I haven't even said anything yet!'

'Stop trying to confuse me,' said Haranga, even though it was himself, confusing himself, basically. 'Tell me where they are or I'll squidge you!'

'You'll what?'

'I'll squidge you. Like this...'

And Haranga, keeping his beady eyes on Steady George – knowing he was the boss man, the guy who made things happen – picked up Black-Eyed Pete in one paw and started squeezing him till the buttons popped off his shirt, the zip broke on his trousers and the dark glasses shot clear off his nose, hit the wall opposite and fell to the ground in a crumpled mess.

'Help! Help! The brightness!' cried Pete. He wasn't too fussed about the zip or the buttons, but he hated – just HATED – losing his sunglasses. His natural state was darkness, and sharp bursts of light made him feel like a vampire might feel when suddenly exposed to the dazzling daylight. 'My shades! My shades!'

'Oh, don't be silly, Pete, stop fussing,' said his boss, unsympathetically. 'It's a cloudy day and you're in a dark alley.'

Haranga put him down, and Pete crawled off to try and find his precious sunglasses, quivering like a mass of custard.

'Your turn now, George?' Haranga offered, reaching out to squidge him.

'No thanks,' said the villain, not much fancying being squished to a pulp. 'Leave me alone, and I'll tell you where your friends are.'

'Go on then,' said Haranga, standing back. 'Tell me.'

'They're nowhere!'

'Nowhere! Of course they're not nowhere!' Haranga gave him a gentle squeeze, just a taster to let him know what was in store if he didn't co-operate, and Steady George's hat flew off his head.

'Stop, stop! I'm telling the truth!'

'Of course you're not telling the truth. Nobody's nowhere. They've got to be somewhere. Now tell me where it is!'

'Well, yes, I suppose they are somewhere,' the villain conceded. 'But it's an in-between sort of place. The sort of place that doesn't really exist.'

'An in-between sort of place?' said Haranga, puzzled. 'In between where and where, exactly.'

'Well…' said George, finding it all a bit difficult to explain, especially to a ten-ton horror, holding him in his grip. 'I don't really know, to tell you the truth. It's neither here nor there. Just somewhere else.'

'What? You're not making any sense. In fact, I think you're trying to trick me, Steady George, and if there's one thing I hate, it's being tricked!' Haranga gave him another little squeeze, just for luck. And Steady George's gold buttons popped off.

'No, really,' said the gangster. 'They're somewhere in the never-never. Somewhere no one's ever been. Somewhere I invented.'

'What are you talking about?' Haranga was losing his patience. 'You're talking rubbish, that's what you're talking!'

'No, no! I'm not. Really. Truly. I mean, I should know. I'm the one who put them there.'

'I don't believe a word of it!' Haranga roared, squeezing Steady George for real this time, deep down in his stomach, till the villain's breakfast found its way back up to his mouth and he couldn't talk for fear of it spraying out all over Haranga. Which was hardly likely to please his oppressor. Or make him lessen the pressure.

'But whatever you've done with them, you'd better get them back here quick, or you're finished!' Haranga continued. And he loosened his grip, then, to give George a chance to go and do something about it.

'But I can't! I keep telling you, they're trapped in the SuperHighway,' said the gangster, once his guts had settled and he felt safe to open his mouth again. Then, realising he wasn't being held, he ran and hid round the back of Jimmy's wheelie bin, where Haranga couldn't reach him. 'I took over Bun's controls and called them through...' he boasted, regaining his confidence.

'You've been there! You've met Bun!'

'Yes,' said George. 'But I switched the system off before the transfer was complete. They're lost in the ether. They don't exist any more!'

'Don't exist?'

'I'm afraid not,' said George, twisting and turning to keep out of Haranga's reach. 'It's my revenge for the way you and your friends treated Pete and me in Dizzy Belle's...'

'You mean when we soggy porridged, mashed potatoed, tomato sauced, baked-beaned, salt and vinegarred, bangers and mashed, omelette and chipped, ham and egged and streaky baconed you?' said Haranga, with a grin, remembering what fun they'd all had.

'Exactly,' replied Steady George, unsmilingly. It hadn't been a lot of fun for him and Pete. 'And it's my revenge for when you bounced Black-Eyed Pete into my stomach outside Barry Frizzle's and then tried to put the squeeze on me. But I got the better of you that time, and I will again, you ugly big mug, you!'

'Oh yeah?' Haranga tried to grab him, but his great bulging arms weren't long enough to reach all the way round a full-size wheelie bin.

'Oh yeah!' Steady George was cocky again, now he knew Haranga couldn't get him. 'Because I've placed your precious little garden gnomes right out of the picture, and there's not a single thing you can do about it.'

'WHAT?!' A voice screamed from the top of Nita's wall. It was Jimmy's grandad. He'd been asleep in Nita's garden and been woken up by all the yelling. 'What did I hear you say? Did I hear you say you've killed my little friends?'

And, without waiting for an answer or an explanation, for he was an impulsive sort of a guy, Grandad took out the pot of particularly gloopy cold porridge that he kept under his jacket for just such a rainy day, and schlooped it all over Steady George –

'Schloo—

ooooo—

ooooo—

ooooo—

oooooop!'

All wet and horrible, flat on his head with a splat, leaving the chief hoodlum paralysed in a paroxysm of horror (just as effective as the Stroke, but a whole heap nastier).

And then slowly, slowly, ever so slowly, it dribbled down over his eyes, his ears, his nose and his mouth, trickled down his neck, front and back, and found its way under his collar and into his shirt, then under his shirt and into his vest, under his vest and onto the hairs on his chest and sticking itself to his sweaty body, all mixing up into a great congealed and gloopy gunk. Lovely! Absolutely lovely!

'Eeeeee—
eeeeeee—
eeeeeee—'

'Yuckkk!' cried George, wiping his hands down his face to try and clear away at least some of the porridge. But managing only to help spread it all over his jacket and down onto his trousers and shoes.

And Haranga took the opportunity to lift him up, pop him in the wheelie bin, wheel him through into Nita's shed and lock it tight. 'That's

Steady George taken care of, then!' he said, wiping his hands in delight.

And it was.

For now.

17

A LOAD OF MEANWHILES

Meanwhile, Black-Eyed Pete managed to slip away down the alley in the dark without anyone noticing. It was nice to be able to let the boss face the music on his own, for once. Well, for twice, actually, considering much the same thing had happened outside Barry Frizzle's. In fact, come to think of it, he was beginning to make quite a habit of it.

He made his way back to Barry Frizzle's, climbed up the ladder – which the teenage sneakthief had managed to purloin from a building site and carry home, pretending to be a late-night window cleaner – and the two of them spent the rest of a long and unjolly night sitting cross-legged on the floor (the police had taken the stolen sofa away), watching shadows move across the wall (the police had also relieved BF of the pilfered television, not to mention the curtains, the light bulbs and the electricity supply, which had been disconnected as he hadn't paid the bill for months), drinking not a single drop of beer (all the local pubs and off-licences had barred him, once the police had informed the owners of their suspicions as to who it was had been ripping them off) and eating not a single forkful of sweet and sour or any other tasty Asian delicacy. For the same applied to Chinese restaurants – they'd resolved not to let BF in the door, ever again).

So, once morning came, it was back down the ladder for both of them and off to Dizzy Belle's to beg her for breakfast. Which, kind-hearted as she always was – as long as you asked her nicely – she was willing to provide. More fool her.

'But you'd better pay me,' she warned them. 'When you get the money, you'd better pay me.'

'I will, Dizzy. I swear, on my grandmother's grave…'

'Sure, Dizz. I promise on my poor Poppa's coffin…'

Yeah, yeah.

*

Meanwhile, Nita's still at home in bed, where she was the last time we saw her. She'd heard a bit of a wild rumpus out in the garden (as Black-Eyed Pete and Steady George fell through the chequerboard, remember) but when she ran to the window there was nothing to see, so she'd gone back to sleep. And even though all sorts of stuff's been happening in the amadan world since then, it doesn't take up more than a few minutes' human time, which I know is a bit weird but that's how it goes. So she's still fast asleep.

Ditto Partho, in the next room. Dream a little dream.

Ditto Jimmy, next door. Snore a snorty snore.

Not ditto Jimmy's dad, who's burning the midnight oil, head bent over his computer, well into his second packet of chocolate biscuits and desperately seeking inspiration. Yet again. Munch, munch.

Not ditto *his* dad – Jimmy's dotty old grandad – either, who, as we've just seen, couldn't sleep a wink and was out on porridge patrol. Well, if Haranga's gone and banjaxed the Stroke, has to be out and about in the dark of night, trying to keep all that badness under control, so it might as well be a thousand-and-six-year-old ex-ghostbuster, mightn't it?

And not ditto the reformed and rehabilitated rapscallion, Haranga, either, who was out there too, of course. Trying to make amends for all the trouble he'd caused. By giving Steady George a good seeing-to. As we already know.

Meanwhile, in Queen Alisha's palace, there was time for all sorts of things to happen. Like…

'What in the name of blinkety-blank's going on?' muttered Bun to himself, entering the control room. He'd just returned from lunch and could tell straight away that something was wrong. Forty-two red lights were flashing on the screens, three separate bleeps were bleeping their bleepity heads off, and even a bear of little brain (or a Bun of little courage) could tell just by looking and listening that this was an emergency, with a capital 'E'.

He set to work, and by the time he'd got things under some sort of control he'd realised they were in a right pretty pickle. That not a single amadan was out there on crimestopper duty, which was bad enough, but the ones who *had* been, had disappeared without a trace. Including Dunk, Bun's bestest ever friend. There wasn't a sign of them, not a single dot on a single screen, there, here or anywhere. They were gone, dissolved, dematerialised.

And there was evidence, too, that one (or possibly two) intruders had been in Bun's room while he'd been out to lunch but were nowhere to be found. Intruders who seemed to have discovered the secrets of the SuperHighway. Intruders, in fact, who seemed to know more about it than Bun himself.

This was a disaster! A complete and utter disaster!

Queen Alisha agreed. 'This is a complete and utter disaster, Bun! How in the name of the Originator of all Amadans could you have let it happen?'

Bun was close to tears. He slowly unpinned the 'O GoSH' badge from his shirt front and handed it over. 'Here you are, Ma'am,' he said, with a sigh. 'I suppose you'll be wanting to give this to someone else, now.'

The Queen raised her eyebrows, and waited for him to explain.

'I've failed you,' Bun continued. 'Failed everyone. I don't think I can remain as Official

Gatekeeper of the SuperHighway any longer.'

Alisha looked at him long and hard, her anger evaporating. 'Don't be silly, Bun. I need you now more than I've ever needed you. Who else can rescue the amadans we've lost?'

'I don't know.' Bun shook his head. 'I don't know if anyone can. But do you really want me to stay on, ma'am? Do you really think I can help you?'

'I certainly hope so,' said the Queen, emphatically. 'What I want you to do is to go back into that control room and have a jolly good try, for there's no one else round here that knows the ins and outs of the SuperHighway better than you do.'

'Except the intruders,' muttered Bun, dejectedly.

'Possibly,' said the Queen. 'Which is why I will make it my responsibility to find out if they're still here. You make it yours to track down Dunk and the others. Find out where they are and don't rest until they're back here safe and sound. Right?'

'Right, Ma'am. I'll do my best.'

*

And meanwhile, out in the ether…

'Jola! Where are you?' It was Fleur, calling out to her younger brother.

'Fleur! Where are you?' It was Jola, desperate to find his sister.

'Help! Where am I?' It was Dunk, swirling round in nothingness, unable to see, unable to hear, unable to smell or touch or taste or…

Every now and then the quality of nothingness would alter ever so slightly as another swirling amadan came whirling past, coming between Dunk and the source of the eternal emptiness. But by the time he'd sensed they were there, they were gone. By the time he'd tried to reach out and touch them, they'd disappeared. By the time he tried to focus in on them to see if it was Fleur, or Jola (or whoever it might be) they'd faded away into nothingness. And even though he could hear a tiny sort of distressed peeping sound, by the time he'd tried to work out where it was coming from and what it might be trying to say, and by the time he'd tried to say something back, they were gone. Off on another revolution, a never-ending circumference of nowhere.

18
SONYA'S COMING CLOSER

Tracking, tracking, through the snow,
Tracking, tracking, here we go,
Always tracking,
Always tracking,
Always bloomin' tracking!

Sonya, eventually – many weeks after setting off, and half-dead with the cold – arrived at the cave on the side of the Great Mountain, deep in the Netherworld, where Haranga had been living.

'Little brother?' she cried, for she could smell that he'd been there. And she guessed, by the look of the cave, that he was missing her. That he was sorry for running away. That he was lost and lonely and couldn't find his way back to her and that he'd chosen somewhere to hide that reminded him as much as possible of his kind, loving sister and their cosy mountain home.

But when she clambered in, over all the debris and fallen rocks from when the mighty boulder had dropped to the floor of the cave and made the whole roof fall in, she began to panic. Something terrible had happened here. Something dreadful had befallen her poor, darling brother.

'HARANGA!' she screeched, having struggled over the rocks, all the way through to the back of the cave and still not found him. But the reek of him was unmistakable. And she knew, beyond the shadow of a doubt, that it was the reek of fear. 'WHERE ARE YOU, LITTLE BROTHER!'

And the thousand and eight bats, still sleeping there, despite the almost total destruction of their home when the cave collapsed, awoke from their daytime slumbers, fluttered in blind confusion, squeaked their high-pitched squeaks and began driving her out.

'Be quiet, you stupid, blundering mice!' Sonya grumbled, as they careered all around her, dive-bombing her right and left, and shepherding her towards the exit. Despite her discomfort, mind you, she managed to watch out for any clues as to what might have befallen her long-lost brother as she went.

She gasped as she came to the edge of the freezehole, and stared down into the pit at the pile of bones below. 'Surely not...' she whispered. 'Surely, surely not.'

But when she stopped to sniff, she knew it wasn't him. 'I bet you it's something he's eaten, though,' she muttered, stomping away. For she knew what a greedy-guts Haranga was, and how hungry he would have been, not only from the hundred years asleep, but from the long, lonely trek through the mountains. She was pretty hungry herself.

She sniffed around the entrance as she left, more carefully than she had when she arrived, and she could tell now that no one had come or gone for a while. So off she went towards NetherEdge, the town that lay at the foot of the mountain.

There was no snow here, for it was a milder, warmer land and spring was further advanced – but Sonya could guess where her little brother had gone, despite the lack of prints. She knew Haranga better than anyone. She knew he'd be lonely by now, and missing her, and that he was likely to be heading for the nearest town, in search of food, company and adventure.

But she didn't know him as well as she thought she did. For she didn't know that the whole purpose of his escape was to get away from her eternal big-sister bossiness. No, she hadn't the faintest idea that her little brother had headed into NetherEdge with the aim of completely turning the tables on her and becoming the boss of anyone and anything he encountered. No, what she didn't know – what she hadn't an inkling of – was that her baby brother, Haranga, had gone off in search of WORLD DOMINATION!

Past the beautiful silent lake Sonya strode, through the deep and birdful wood, past thriving farms, over burgeoning fields, until she came to the happy, bubbling little town of NetherEdge. For everything had changed in the NetherWorld since we saw it last. No longer was it the dark and dismal place of exile it used to be, for Queen Alisha – now that Jimmy and Nita had helped her to see the error of her ways – had opened all the borders and colour had flooded in, bringing with it warmth and happiness and an influx of more privileged amadans.

'My brother!' muttered Sonya, striding forth into the town. 'My brother is here, and I will find him!'

19

THE POINT OF NO RETURN

The first thing Nita and Jimmy did the morning after the battle with Steady George and Black-Eyed Pete in Dizzy Belle's, was to open up the shed, looking for Haranga.

And there, instead, snoring away beneath a mountain of dried-up porridge, was none other than Steady George himself. He looked so ridiculous, they couldn't help but laugh.

'What do you think he's doing here?' whispered Nita to her friend, once she'd managed to control the giggles.

'Grandad must have got him!' said Jimmy, desperately trying to suppress the sniggers himself. Steady George looked helpless in his sleep, but, even smothered in porridge, he wasn't the sort of person they wanted to meet in a dark alley, or a dark shed, for that matter. So, careful not to wake him, they backed out, locking the door behind them, and went off to find Grandad and ask him what had happened.

The old fellow was still fast asleep too, after his night on the prowl, so they went back over to Nita's to see if they could track down Haranga. Who should have been in the shed, but obviously hadn't wanted to share it with a porridged-up gangster. They found him, eventually, after looking all over the house, under a pile of old carpets in Nita's cellar, resting.

'It must have been a busy night,' said Nita, impressed. 'We'd better leave them all to recover. Let's check in with Bun and see what Dunk and the others are getting up to. I suppose they must have gone back home after we gave Pete and George a good scare down in Dizzy Belle's, for there's no sign of them round here.'

Dot dot dot dot, dit dit dit dit, dot dot dot, beep beep beep beep beep, hissssssssssssssssssssssssssss. Click on 'home' to find the search engine. Type in www.amadansanonymous.com.

'Hi, Bun.' Nita beamed as the Official

Gatekeeper's pointy features began appearing on the screen in front of her. 'Did Fleur and the others get back safely last night?' But her smile slipped as she noticed the look on his face.

'You don't know?' said the traumatised amadan.

'Know what?'

'They're gone. Disappeared off the face of the universe.'

'What do you mean?'

So Bun explained about the intruders and how they'd somehow managed to gain control of the SuperHighway, recall all the amadans who'd been out on crimestopping duty, and fire them off into the ether.

Nita was horrified. And furious. 'It must have been Steady George, getting his revenge!' she raged, for she'd taken an instant dislike to the overweight gangster the first time she'd seen him. 'It's just the sort of foul and horrible thing he would do.'

She was very fond of Fleur, never mind Jola and Dunk. She couldn't bear to think of them confined to an eternity of endless wandering. 'I'm going back to that shed to find out what he's done with them and how to get them back!'

'What shed?' asked Bun. 'What are you talking about?'

And Nita explained about finding Steady George only a few minutes earlier, fast asleep and covered in porridge. 'And you can be sure his sidekick, Black-Eyed Pete, is round here somewhere, too. There's no way he'd hang about over in your place without his boss.'

Bun, once he was convinced that Steady George was the culprit, and that he was safely locked up in Nita's shed after an attack of the Grandads, was mightily relieved. The intruders were no longer in amadan land, so as soon as Jimmy and Nita signed off he got straight through to Alisha and told her what he'd discovered.

'Excellent,' said the Queen. 'Pass on my congratulations to Jimmy's grandad for capturing him, next time you speak to him. But more importantly and very urgently, Bun, I need you to find out how those two villains got here, and then do whatever you have to in order to make sure it can NEVER happen again.'

So Bun put all his efforts over the next hour or two, amadan-time, into thoroughly investigating the chequerboard transference process and, once he'd come to grips with how it worked, he put a complete and total block on it – put a bomb under it, basically – so that no one could ever get through it, either way, again.

'You know the monitors in your garden, Nita?' said Bun, when she came back from trying, and failing, to wake Steady George, who was stuck fast in the deepest, stickiest sleep he'd ever known. 'I want you to put them all away. I've made sure they can't be used any more, so you might as well give them back to your dad.'

'But I can't,' said Nita, shaking her head. 'It's the only way for Haranga to get home, remember. Surely you don't want him to be stuck here for ever?'

There was a long silence. Bun sat, stock still, until Nita, watching him, thought the line must be down. Then, 'Ah,' said the little amadan, passing his hand over his face as he realised the terrible mistake he'd made. The second terrible mistake. 'I hadn't thought of that.'

And, without telling Queen Alisha, for he couldn't bear to face her disapproval yet again, he shut himself away to investigate whether it was possible to re-open the lines one last time, to get Haranga home. But it wasn't. The connections were destroyed. There was absolutely no way to reconnect them.

So, apart from the ones who'd been cast into the darkness, the amadans were safe from Steady George. But Jimmy, Nita and the whole of the human world were stuck with one misplaced enormity: the slightly-less-horrendous-than-he-used-to-be-but-still-not-the-most-desirable-person-to-have-knocking-about-the-place, Haranga.

20

THE INCREDIBLE SHRINKING HULKS

'You know what?' said Barry Frizzle to his mate, Black-Eyed Pete, as they sat polishing off their meal at Dizzy Belle's.

'What?' said Pete, licking the plate clean with his tongue. He always was a disgusting eater, was Pete.

'You're shrinking!'

'I'm what?'

'You're shrinking! I'm sure you've lost at least a foot since we came in here.'

Black-Eyed Pete pulled back his chair and looked down at his shoes. 'No,' he said, wiggling them both. 'They're all present and correct.'

'No, I mean a foot in height, stupid!' said Barry. And then he gasped, realising that he'd never have dared address Pete in such a way, if the hardman gangster had been his usual intimidating self.

'Who are you calling "stupid", stupid?' Pete's hackles were rising. Though not as high as they used to rise, now he was shrinking.

Dizzy Belle came in from the kitchen, hearing the raised voices. 'Hey Pete,' she joked, in that practised way she had of calming things down. 'You're the first person to lose weight from eating my breakfasts!'

'I've lost weight?'

'Yeah,' said Dizzy, looking him up and down. Mainly down. 'You're about half the size you were when you came in.'

Black-Eyed Pete stood up, then. And realised that they weren't just having him on. There was no doubt about it, his clothes were hanging off him. He was decidedly diminished.

'Help!' he said, panicking. 'What am I going to do?'

Dizzy and Frizzle both shrugged. They weren't too bothered, as a matter of fact. Black-Eyed Pete had always been too big for his boots, so it was nice to see him being brought down a peg or two, for once.

'Come with me, Baz!' cried a desperate Pete, pulling his co-breakfaster to his feet and rushing to the door. 'I'm off to find the boss. Maybe he'll know what to do.'

When Nita, with Jimmy in tow, plucked up the courage to go and confront Steady George in the shed, to demand that he release Fleur and the other amadans from their perpetual wanderings, they got a heck of a shock. He was tiny!

'Help!' the gangster squeaked. 'I've been shrunk by all that blasted porridge!'

And when Haranga arrived on the scene, fresh from his dozings (not sleepings, exactly, as he only slept once in a hundred years, but every now and again he needed a bit of shut-eye, in between), everyone stared at him, goggle-eyed. Because even he – he of the infamous immensity – was titchy! Well, titchy in comparison to the incredible bulk he used to be, anyway.

And when Black-Eyed Pete, with Barry Frizzle in tow, came to investigate what his boss was up to and to seek his advice on how to get his size back, Nita took one look at him and put two and two together.

'It's not the effect of the porridge,' she said,

grinning at their discomfort. 'It can't be, for there's three of you shrinking, and only one of you was Grandadded.'

'So what is it, if it's not the porridge, Clever-clogs?' asked George, deeply disgruntled. Never mind deeply uncomfortable, as anyone would be, having spent a night in a shed covered in cold porridge, which had now dried into a crusty, caked-on, coagulated coating.

'Yeah, what's it all about?' asked Haranga, extremely annoyed, also. He liked being big, did Haranga. Even if he was trying to be a bit nicer these days, big was what he did, basically.

'Yeah, spill the beans, kid,' said Black-Eyed Pete, who didn't fancy a lifetime of unemployment, for who was likely to take on a miniscule hardman? 'What's going on?'

'It's the chequerboard,' said Nita, always the first to work things out. 'You all came through the grid, it filled you full of gaps, and now you're leaking through the holes. To put it bluntly, guys,' she said, grinning, 'you're fading away.'

Because what all three of them had forgotten about was how, when they'd transferred through Nita's dad's monitors, all laid out in the garden with gaps between the screens, it had created gaps in themselves, too. So that Haranga had become ninety percent monster and ten percent invisibility, like a patchwork quilt version of himself that hadn't been sewn together yet.

'Hey, maybe the kid's right,' said Pete, nodding. 'It's like when I told you there were lines all over you, Boss, just after we'd arrived in that weird garden-gnome place. It was like you'd been taken apart and put back together, only it hadn't worked properly.'

'Mmmm,' said George. It was all coming back to him. 'Like we'd been unzipped into squares and laid out side by side, like Scrabble boards, or crossword puzzles or chessboards or whatever. I'd sort of got used to it. Didn't think any more about it, to tell you the truth.'

'Me too,' said Pete.

'Me three,' said Haranga.

'Yeah, well the effect was dormant for a while, just lines, nothing more, but now, like I said, you're leaking,' explained Nita. 'You're going to get smaller and smaller till you disappear altogether!'

'What can we do? How can we prevent it?' asked all three at the same time, realising the immensity (or maybe lack of immensity) of the problem, and hoping for a clever-clogs answer.

Which is what Nita had at the ready, of course. 'You can't prevent it,' she said, shrugging her shoulders. She waited, then, to watch the looks of disappointment wash across their fading-away faces, and then added, 'Not unless you apologise for your misdeeds and agree to live a life of unadulterated goodness from here on out.'

She'd no idea if this was the case, in fact, but she thought it was worth a go.

'But I've done that already!' protested Haranga. 'I'm a reformed monstrosity!'

'True,' said Nita, nodding at him. 'So maybe if you give it time you'll be OK. But what about you two?' she asked Pete and George. 'Are you willing to do the same? To turn your backs on a lifetime of crime and general out-and-out badness?'

'What's the option?' said George, curling his lip at the thought.

'Invisibility,' said Nita. 'Getting smaller and smaller till you're of no size, no worth, and you've disappeared for ever down the plughole of emptiness.'

'Hmmm,' said George, not liking the sound of that at all. 'Not much choice, then. And what happens if we say yes?'

'We'll connect up with Bun and see if he can work out how to stop the shrinking.'

'That computer whizz, over in garden-gnome-land?'

'The very man.'

'And will he be able to get us back to normal size?'

'Maybe,' replied Nita, smiling. She hadn't a clue if Bun would really be able to do it, but she thought it was worth a try. 'If we're convinced you mean it.'

'And will you keep that crazy wrinkled old porridge-flinger away?' asked George, looking round to check that Grandad hadn't crept up, unannounced, bowl in hand.

'Yes, we'll tell your grandad to keep his secret weapon under wraps, won't we, Jimmy?' said Nita.

Jimmy nodded.

'So is it a deal?' asked Nita.

Pete and George looked at each other.

'It's a deal,' they said, unenthusiastically, realising they hadn't really any option other than to make the best of a bad job. By agreeing to give up the bad job. If you get my meaning.

'Oh, one other thing…' added Nita, as another thought suddenly crossed her mind. 'Before we can plug the gaps and stop you disappearing…'

'What's that?' asked George, waiting to hear the small print.

'Well, it's not very nice, the idea of fading to nothingness. Is it?'

'No,' agreed George. 'It's not.'

'Well, that's exactly what you've done to my friend Fleur!'

'And Jola!' said Jimmy.

'And Dunk!' added Haranga. 'And all the other crimestopping amadans!'

'Exactly,' said Nita. 'So unless you agree to get them back, there's no way we're going to help you. Fair enough?'

'Doh,' said George, realising he wasn't in any position to argue. 'Fair enough.'

So Fleur connected up with Bun. 'I've got Steady George here. He wants to speak to you.'

Bun was horrified. 'That evil baggage! There's no way I'd even spit on him, never mind talk to him, after what he's done!'

But Nita explained what had happened, and that George had said he was looking for forgiveness. 'He wants to work with you to rescue Dunk and the others. And, in return, I said we'd try to plug the gaps that are making him shrink.'

'Do you trust him?'

'Not entirely. He's only doing it out of self-interest, not because he's seen the error of his ways. But I think we've got to give it a try, anyway. He's obviously a bit of a computer whizz himself, and that's what we need to get them back.'

Bun was silent. And hurt.

'Oh, Bun,' said Nita, apologetically. 'I know you're the REAL computer whizz, it's just that Steady George probably knows a bit more about how Dunk and the others were spun off into nothingness, given that he was the one who actually did it...'

'Oh, all right, then,' said Bun, grumpily. 'Put him on.'

21

HUGS AND HONOURS

Crime was running rife, now the amadans were out of action. It had been bad enough while the Stroke was in decline, but now that they'd all been blasted off the face of the earth, into goodness knows where, things were going from bad to worse.

Bike theft, cat burgling, breaking and entering, foul play, dirty work, hanky-panky, gang rule – you name it, in some shady corner it was happening. And just as Haranga had predicted when he'd gone and started this whole crazy shenanigans, law and order was in danger of breaking down altogether.

Something had to be done, and Bunsen Bernard and Steady George agreed to put their differences aside and see if they could do it.

But time was ticking by and things weren't looking good for the poor abandoned amadans. Things weren't looking good at all.

'Jola! Where are you?'

'Fleur! Where are you?'

'Help, where am I?'

Round and round for ever they went, endlessly, aimlessly circling each other in the eternal unforgiving emptiness. Unable to see, hear, smell, touch, taste… Unable to think anything other than sheer total panic, anything other than, 'I'm an amadan! Get me out of here!'

And then, suddenly, bang! They're back in the control room!

'Bun? Is that you?' Dunk's blinking, shielding his eyes from the sudden and dazzling brightness. But Bun's all over him, hugging him like a long-lost teddy bear.

'You're back!' cried his bestest-ever friend, little bunny tears dribbling down his face.

Jola and Fleur were hard at it too, blinking away and trying to figure out where they were and what had happened.

'I thought I'd lost you for ever,' cried Fleur,

holding her brother tightly.

'You had,' said Jola, massively relieved to be back in the world of reality. 'And I'd lost you.'

And all the other crimestopper amadans who'd been out on duty that night – all twenty-seven of them, as it turned out – each did the same. Blink, blink. Jump for joy. Hug, huggity, hug.

'We did it!' cried Bun, through the channels of transference to his friends in the shed. 'They're here!'

And everyone cheered, even Steady George. It's funny how doing something good for someone can give you a warm feeling in the cockles of your heart sometimes. Even when you're an out-an-out, sworn-to-badness, no-good gangster.

Haranga hugged Pete. Barry Frizzle hugged Grandad, who'd just arrived on the scene, having at last awoken from a deep and dreamy sleep (BF having first checked that the old fellow didn't have any porridge concealed anywhere upon his personage – he didn't want it to squidge out all over him). Jimmy hugged Nita, which he'd never normally do, not with anyone watching, anyway.

And, back in the control room in the palace of the amadans, Queen Alisha – who'd given orders to be told the very second anything of any importance happened – rushed in and proceeded to hug everyone there, too. Jumping up and down and squealing with delight. Very unqueenly behaviour altogether, but she loved her people, did Alisha, and she simply couldn't bear for any of them to come to any harm.

'I'd like to thank you, Mr George...' she began, seating herself down at the controls, once she was all hugged out. For Steady George was deserving of thanks, having worked incredibly hard with Bun for what seemed like ages to find a way to bring the strandees-in-nowhereness back to somewhere real. Well, relatively real, anyway.

'Just call me George, your Highness,' replied the gangster, embarrassed at being made a fuss of, but secretly rather delighted. 'There's no need to use a title.'

'Actually, I won't just call you George,' answered the Queen, his response giving her an idea for how to reward him for his efforts. 'Because you were willing to turn your back on badness in order to help me recover my trusted amadans from the eternal abyss...' she proclaimed, in a regal voice.

Then she remembered his role in the affair.

'Even though it WAS you who put them there,' she added, with a slight edge in her voice…

'From now on, you shall be known in the amadan world as…Sir George!'

'Sir George!' said Steady, dumbfounded at the honour. And mightily, mightily pleased. In fact, so pleased that a big fat dribble of happiness welled up in the corner of his eye and trickled down through the crusty old porridge. It was the first tear he'd dribbled since his pet bunny rabbit, Hopsadaisy, had been run over by an out-of-control milk cart on Wheelbarrow Hill, at the age of four and three quarters. George was four and three quarters, that is. Not Hopsadaisy. Or the milk cart. Or Wheelbarrow Hill.

'Hey,' said Haranga, shoving Sir George aside and plunking himself down in front of the screen. 'That's not fair, Ma'am! He only did it to save his skin. He only did it so someone would plug the gaps and stop him leaking. He only did it because he doesn't want to become a titch of a thing, and lose all of his powers of intimidation. It's not as though he's going to stop being bad for ever, like I am.'

'You never can tell,' said the Queen, with a knowing little smile. 'Maybe you don't want to be an out-and-out, sworn-to-badness, no-good gangster till the end of your live-long days, Sir George? Maybe the warm feeling in the cockles of your heart from doing something good for once might make you stop and think before you return to your evil ways, mightn't it, Sir George?'

Her words were met by a silence from the newly beknighted villain. A lingering, quizzical silence.

'But anyway,' the Queen continued. 'So you fancy a title yourself, Haranga?' She knew the monster was being rather rude, questioning her judgement, but she could understand the point he was making and she was in a generous mood.

'Well, now you mention it…' said the monster.

'Fair enough, my friend,' said Alisha. 'For services to the amadans and because you have made a complete, total and for ever reformation from bad guy to good…' she gave him a long hard look, 'I hereby proclaim you…'

A hush filled the shed.

'Viscount Haranga!'

'Viscount Haranga!' the monster whispered, deeply impressed. And then he pointed a fat stubby finger at his less-capacious-than-usual chest. 'Look at me, everyone! I'm a viscount!'

'What about me?' said Black-Eyed Pete, never

one to want to miss out when there were goodies on offer. 'Do I get one of your fancy titles, Ma'am?' he asked, pushing his face into the screen.

'Will you be good?' said Alisha, studying his features for signs of contrition. 'For ever?'

'For ever's an awful long time, Ma'am,' muttered Pete. 'But I suppose I could try…if you make it worth my while…'

'Fair enough,' said Alisha, deciding, as she was in such a good mood, to ignore his shifty impertinence. 'Kneel on the floor there.' Pete got down on his knees, and then the Queen announced, over the airwaves, in her most regal voice, 'Arise, Duke Pete!'

'Duke Pete!' Pete was beaming like a babe-in-arms. 'That's the nicest thing anyone's ever called me!'

'How about me?' said Barry Frizzle, wondering if there was any chance he could get in on the act. I mean, if all the bad guys were getting gongs, then why shouldn't he? 'Do I get one of these Dukenesses?' he said, edging Pete aside.

'Will you promise to be good?' asked the Queen, her generosity still on overdrive, her faith in the powers of forgiveness (taught to her by Jimmy and Nita), still strong. For she still remembered the time, way back, when Haranga himself had been a terrible tyrant, much worse than any of these. They'd cornered him, and had him at their mercy, but young Jimmy had taken pity on the horrendous horror, saved his life, and convinced the Queen to give the dreaded monster a chance to redeem himself.

'I'll have a go,' said Baz, looking round the shed at all the doubters. 'I'll try anything once, me,' he told them.

'Kneel, then,' instructed the Queen.

Barry knelt, his knees sinking into the drippy porridge on the floor of the shed.

'Arise, Baronet Barry.'

'Baronet Barry! Wow!'

And, with that, Sir George, Viscount Haranga, Duke Pete and Baronet Barry took each other by the hand and ran out into the garden, hopping and skipping, where they did a Dance of Distinction, all around the edge of the lawn. (The middle was covered in computer screens, for some strange reason.)

After which, Steady George was allowed into Nita's house to wash off all the dried-on porridge and to borrow Nita's dad's pyjamas while his clothes went through the wash.

'Can I borrow your jammies, Dad?'

'Of course you can, my dearest daughter. As I've always said, you can have anything you like, and do anything you like, as long as it does no harm to life nor limb.'

See, no questions asked. The perfect sort of dad, isn't he? Just lets you get on with it.

And would you believe it, but the bestowal of titles upon them made them so inordinately proud – Viscount Haranga, Duke Pete and Sir George – that they puffed themselves up so much over the course of the rest of the day, that they not only began to regain all their lost weight, but they sealed the gaps in their overall structure caused by the chequerboard transference process, too, till they were well on their way to being back to normal, only better. Not any bigger than they'd been to begin with, which was quite big enough, thank you very much (in Haranga and Steady George's case, anyway) but definitely better. For now, at least.

And the only problem left, now all that was sorted, was how to get Haranga back to the world of the amadans. It was OK having him over on the human side of the pond for a while – Jimmy, Nita and Grandad rather enjoyed his company – but really, he was far too big and outlandish to survive here long without drawing attention to himself. And once he drew attention to himself, there was no telling what sort of problems might ensue.

So it was time to get him home. Now, how in the name of goodness are we going to do that?

22

HARANGA IN THE BATH

'Stop!' cried Bun.

'Stop what?' yelled Nita.

'Stop growing!'

'Stop growing?'

'Yes, stop growing!'

'But why?' said Nita, who hadn't a clue what he was on about. She'd just reconnected, to see if there was any news from the amadans, and there was her old friend, Bunsen Bernard, the Official Gatekeeper of the SuperHighway, screaming and yelling at her. 'Why should I stop growing?' she repeated.

'Not you! Haranga!'

'Haranga?'

'Yes, Haranga!' cried an exasperated Bun.

'But why?' asked Nita, again. She wasn't getting the hang of this conversation, not one little bit.

'Because that's the only way we're going to get him back where he belongs,' answered Bun. 'I've been thinking about it for ages, and I've come up with the obvious solution.'

'Which is…?' It was early in the morning, and Nita was somewhat less quick on the uptake than she usually was.

'Which is, that if he's still only about the size of an amadan, or Jimmy or Nita, anyway, then he'll be able to fit through the SuperHighway. We don't need all that special system of screens you used before.'

'You're right!' said Nita, understanding at last. 'Now why didn't I think of that?'

So she ran to the shed and there was Haranga, definitely bigger than he'd been the night before but still not much bigger than her or Jimmy or Grandad.

'Haranga, Haranga, stop!' she yelled at him.

'Stop what?' said the diminutive monster, wiping the doziness from his eyes. It's not very nice, being brought back to the surface by someone yelling 'Stop!' at you.

'Stop growing!' cried Nita.

'What do you mean, "stop growing"?' said

Haranga, frowning. 'One minute everyone wants me to return to my normal size. The next minute they're coming in here at ten to cockcrow, or whatever ridiculous hour it is, and yelling at me to stop. I mean, make up your minds!'

'We *did* want you to grow,' said Nita. 'But now we don't.' And she explained to the poor confused half-asleep mini-monster about Bun's plan.

'Fair enough,' said Haranga, once he understood. He liked being with Jimmy and Nita but he knew he couldn't stay there for ever. Full size, he just didn't fit in. 'But don't you think it's maybe too late? Don't you think I'm too big already? I mean, I'm growing all the time. There's nothing I can do to stop it.'

So Nita waved her arms in the air, calling for silence, and put her brainwaves in gear. And in next to no time she had it sorted.

'I've got it!' she said. And she led him out to her wheelie bin, pushed it over to the wall, got Haranga to climb up on the bin, then up onto the wall, then lean over and open the lid of the bin, and then drop himself in.

'Are you sure?' said Haranga, as she explained the plan.

'I'm sure,' said Nita.

'Can we take the rubbish out first?'

'We can take the rubbish out first.'

Once Haranga was in, Nita clambered up onto the wall and jumped down on the lid, so it was pressing down on his head, and he was wedged in tight.

'It's not very comfortable,' came a muffled moan from inside.

'It's not supposed to be,' said Nita, jumping up and down a bit more to make sure he couldn't grow while he was in there.

'And it's a bit smelly,' complained a muffled Haranga.

'Yeah, sorry about that,' said Nita, 'but it shouldn't be for long. You stay here, while I go and call Bun back up.'

She hopped back down to the ground and ran back through to the computer.

Dot dot dot dot, dit dit dit dit, dot dot dot, beep beep beep beep beep, hissssssssssssssssssssssssssssss. Click on 'home' to find the search engine. Type in www.amadansanonymous.com.

'Right,' she said, when Bun appeared. 'We're all ready to roll. I've squashed Haranga in the wheelie bin so he can't get any bigger. See if you can get him across.'

So Bun switched on the SuperHighway Transference Process and summoned him home.

But nothing happened.

He tried again.

And still nothing happened.

He tried one more time, and all that came up on his screen was the message, 'Item too large to transport.'

'It's no good,' he told Nita. 'He's already too big. I afraid you're stuck with him.'

But then Nita called for silence again, closed her eyes tight and focused on her brainwaves. And it worked! She was getting back into clever-clogs mode now she was fully awake.

'We'll stick him in the bath, that's what we'll do!' she cried. 'If we leave him in there long enough and hot enough, he's sure to shrink.'

'Are you sure?' said Bun.

'I'm sure,' said Nita.

So she went outside, to tell Haranga. And found her wheelie bin on its side in the yard.

'Get me out!' yelled Haranga, his head poking out of the top.

'What happened?' she asked him.

'I fell over,' said Haranga.

So Nita tugged and she pulled, she pulled and

she tugged, and eventually she managed to get him out.

'No luck with Bun?' said the smelly monster, once he'd dusted himself down.

'I'm afraid not,' said Nita, shaking her head. 'But I've just had another brainwave.' She wrinkled her nose. He didn't half smell whiffy. 'It's just what you need right now, in more ways than one.'

'I hope it's not another wheelie bin?' said Haranga, unenthusiastically.

'Oh no,' said Nita. 'It's much nicer than that. We're going to give you a bath! If you stay in the water long enough, maybe you'll shrink.'

'A bath? What's a bath?'

So Nita took him upstairs, ran the water nice and hot, squeezed in a whole bottle of bubble bath, and encouraged him to climb in. Haranga didn't much like the idea. He'd never had a bath before in his life, and he couldn't even see the water for bubbles, but once he was in, he found it really rather cosy, and a lot less smelly than a wheelie bin.

Nita showed him how to top it up, whenever it ran cold, and then she left him to it. 'Feel free to use the soaps,' she said, as she left.

Haranga lay there, luxuriating in the warmth.

This is the life, he thought. A whole heap better than living in a cave on a dusty mountain. He picked up the plastic ducks, and raced them through the bubbles. Then he had a look at the line of bottles, and decided to give them a try. First he took the chamomile shampoo and rubbed it into his hair. Then he tried the mango butter, the bergamot body wash and the Mediterranean olive body scrub (with exfoliating walnut shell) and rubbed them in all over, too. Then he spotted another bottle on the floor and gave himself a good squirt of ecological pine fresh toilet cleaner. Mmmmm, he smelled delicious!

And there he lay, for a good two and a half hours, chucking stuff on, rinsing it off, chucking it on, rinsing it off, till he'd squeezed every last drop out of every last pot (including the toothpaste, which he rubbed into his feet to make them nice and minty). Topping the bath up with hot water every time it started to get cold, until there was no more hot, and his skin was all shrivelled up.

('Nita, is there someone in the bathroom?'

'Yes, Dad. It's just one of my friends. They won't be long.')

('Nita, is that drip coming through from upstairs?'

('Yes, Dad. Sorry, Dad. I'll go and fetch a bucket.')

('Nita, has your friend used all the hot water?'
'Yes, Dad. Sorry, Dad. He was a bit dirty.')

('Dad! Can my friend borrow your bathrobe?'
'Yes, dear. Of course they can, dear.')

'That's better,' said Nita, when Haranga came to the bathroom door at last – she'd been knocking for ages – all towelled and wrinkled, shampooed, soaped and powdered. In fact he'd never been so clean and so fresh in his whole life.

'Am I smaller?' he asked.

And he was! Massively smaller! 'Yes!' cried Nita, 'You've shrunk!' And then she noticed the debris of wet towels, empty bottles and flooded floor. 'Massively cleaner, too!'

So they called up Bun again. He switched on the SuperHighway, tried summoning Haranga home, and this time it worked!

One minute he was standing there, in front of Nita, all bright and sparkling, and the next minute he was sitting next to Bun in the control room, emanating all sorts of interesting odours.

'Well, well,' said the Gatekeeper, looking him up and down. 'It's amazing what a short time on earth can do. You've certainly changed!'

'How do you mean?' asked the monster.

'For one thing,' said Bun, 'you're a whole heap smaller than when I last saw you…'

'Yes,' agreed Haranga. 'But I'll grow again now, won't I?'

'Hopefully,' said Bun. 'And for another thing, you're a whole lot prettier.'

'Prettier?' Haranga raised his eyebrows. Now that he was back home again, he wasn't too sure looking pretty was such a good idea. I mean, he had a reputation to protect.

'Oh yes,' said Bun, sniffing the air all around him. 'I've never seen you so pretty. Or smelling so fresh.'

23

KIDNAPPED

'Viscount Haranga!' It was Alisha, rushing into the control room to greet him. 'I'm delighted to have you back. And how sweet-smelling!'

Haranga liked the title, and the warmth of the Queen's greeting. But he was rapidly going off the idea of being quite *so* sweet-smelling. It had been fun at the time, splashing about in his first ever bath, but somehow it didn't seem quite right, being so clean and fragrant, so soaped and shampooed, now he was back in the real world. Somehow, it wasn't the appropriate image for a foul and horrendous monster, even a reformed one.

'Let's have a party!' cried the Queen, clapping her hands. 'To celebrate your safe return, my

Viscount, and that of all my amadans who were abandoned in space.'

'Great idea, Ma'am,' said Bun, who liked nothing better than a good knees-up. 'We'll have sticky buns and elderbox, and I'll get my friends, the Five Fiery Fiddlers, to come and lead the dancing!'

'Can we ask Jimmy over?' suggested Haranga.

'Of course,' said the Queen. 'And Nita.'

'And Jimmy's grandad?' asked Bun. 'It'd be nice to see him again.'

'Most definitely,' said Alisha.

'What about little Partho?' Bun added. 'Do you think it'd be all right if they bring him over, too, Ma'am? I haven't met him yet.'

'Why not?' said the Queen. 'I haven't either, and it'll be nice to have a human here who's smaller than us.'

And so, the very next evening, the party was in full swing, there in the Great Hall.

Jimmy, Nita, Partho, Grandad and all the amadans were having a whale of a time – singing and dancing, eating and drinking, laughing and talking, chuckling and giggling – when a figure appeared at the window, unnoticed. A large and dishevelled figure who'd come to spoil the party.

For it was none other than Sonya, Haranga's abandoned sister, tired, hungry and disgusted. Who had found NetherEdge, when she'd got there, deserted (for everyone had been invited to the party) and so she'd kept on marching, onward and ever angrier, until she'd arrived at the palace. Where she took one look through the window at her big little brother, Haranga, prancing about in the middle of the room in the arms of the Queen of all the amadans, and was appalled, absolutely appalled.

For one thing, he was all clean and tidy, which was utterly unheard of. And for another, he was dancing, which was even more unheard of.

'I've lost him,' hissed the furious Sonya, determining then and there to get her revenge, both on her brother and on everyone who had stolen him away from her. 'Lost him to those nasty little gremlins,' she moaned, in total disgust.

Just then, though, her attention was drawn to the sight of a happy little Partho, running out into the dark and empty courtyard, skipping and laughing.

'A child!' said Sonya, immediately captivated. 'A human child!'

It was the first time she had ever seen one. She knew they came from a far-distant land, much further-distant than this, and her mother, in the years before her parents' disappearance (the years that Haranga had absolutely no memory of, because he was only a babe-in-arms when his momma and pappa had left, sadly never to return), used to tell her stories of a faraway world, peopled by pretty little humans, and even prettier little baby humans.

Oh, those lovely little poppets, with their tiny fingers, their angelic little smiles, their coos and their giggles. In fact, Sonya's mother used to talk so fondly about them that her daughter sometimes wished she was one, so that her very own momma would love her even more.

'If I could have one of those pretty little humans to look after,' her mother used to say, musing to herself when she thought Sonya couldn't hear, 'I'd be happy. So happy.'

So that, on the fateful winter morning when they went out into the snow, never to return, and for many years after that, Sonya thought her parents must have gone off to find themselves a human child to love. That they didn't want to look after a big ugly sister (Sonya) and a great cumbersome lump of a thumb-sucker (Haranga) any more. That they wanted someone sweet and pretty, for once.

And now here was one, right before her! She watched Partho as he danced around the courtyard, and felt a great surge of big-sisterly affection. Not that she was Partho's big sister, of course, but she *was* Haranga's, and he'd gone off and deserted her. Gone off and turned all goody-goody. Gone off and become all lovey-dovey with those sickly-looking amadan creatures. Oooh, it made her want to spit!

And now here was a poor little human child, running about in front of her, all alone and abandoned. A little male, by the look of him. A little boy child, many light years from home, and searching for someone to look after him, just like a big sister should – someone to love him and take care of him and protect him from bright lights and danger.

A little boy child, who'd obviously been kidnapped by those foul and horrible amadan things (Sonya hadn't noticed the other humans in the room), and was desperate to get away from all that fiddly screechy noise on the other side of the window. From all those ugly-looking stomping-about creatures, all jam-packed into one shiny, horrible room. A poor little human boy, all smiling and giggling out there in the yard, because he was so happy to have escaped the evil clutches of those ridiculous goblins at last.

But any second now they'd come out to find him, thought Sonya. Any second now they'd notice he'd gone and come rushing out, in search of him. They'd grab him tight and drag him back into that horrendous scrum she could see through the window – for to someone like Sonya, who'd always lived in the empty wilderness, such a crush of bodies was worse than her worst nightmare – and keep the poor little boy a prisoner for the whole of the rest of his livelong days.

But Sonya, of course, in her loneliness, was completely misunderstanding the situation. Partho was in fact having a totally wonderful time. Ever since Nita had told him he was invited to the party in the Great Hall of the Queen of the Amadans, his feet had barely touched the ground.

Travelling through the SuperHighway had been brill.

('Dad,' said Nita, 'I'm just taking Partho out for a bit.'

'That's fine, dear. I'm sure you'll be sensible.')

Arriving in the control room, meeting Bun, and then good old Haranga again, and then being presented to the beautiful Queen Alisha, had been amazing, truly amazing! And then the party. What a party!

In fact, young Partho was having such an incredible time that he'd decided, in the middle of the action, to go outside, run three times round the courtyard, take a big gulp of fresh air (it was so hot in there!), pinch himself to check if it was real – it WAS real – and then run back inside for another dose of fun and excitement.

So there he was, rushing about the yard, skipping and laughing and singing for joy, when he noticed the window, and decided to pop over to it and surprise all his new friends by waving at them from outside.

But Sonya, unseen and alone, gasped with a mixture of delight and concern when she saw the boy coming close. This was her chance. She must act now, to save the poor little fellow from peril.

'Hello there,' she whispered. And Partho turned round and smiled, thinking, in the darkness that it was Haranga, come out to check on him (for Sonya had the same deep voice as her brother, and the same massive outline).

'Follow me,' she said, as quietly as possible so as neither to scare him nor to alert anyone inside, 'for I have something to show you.' And Partho, who loved secrets, and who had absolutely no reason to doubt that it was Haranga, wishing to share one with him, did exactly as he was told and followed her, out of the grounds of the palace and away.

And nobody saw them. Not one single amadan. Everyone for miles around had been invited to the party, and they were all in the Great Hall, talking and laughing, eating and drinking, singing and dancing, waltzing and salsa-ing, jigging and reeling, scoffing and quaffing, and partaking of puffweed and elderbox in moderation (those who were old enough).

Even the Queen's royal guards had been invited to join in the fun, for now that Haranga and the gangsters had all sworn to goodness, the amadans had no enemies. Not one. So they were all in there, having a ball. And not, for a long, long time, not one of them even thinking of poor little Partho.

24

LITTLE BOY LOST

'Partho! Where are you, Partho?'

Jimmy and Nita had just come off the dance floor, after a particularly strenuous amadan tango, and gone looking for a cold drink to cool them down, when Nita suddenly realised that she hadn't seen her little brother for ages.

Last time she'd looked he'd been over in the games area, playing cops and robbers with Dunk.

'He said he was going out for some fresh air,' Dunk told her, when she found him, standing by the bar with Bun. 'But that was yonks ago. I thought he was with you.'

They searched the room, in and out of the dancers, but Partho was nowhere to be seen, and

Nita was getting more and more worried.

'STOP THE MUSIC!' she finally screamed, springing up onto the stage, all teeth, curls and desperation. And the Five Fiery Fiddlers' bows froze in their hands. 'I'VE LOST PARTHO!' she hollered, to all and sundry. 'My little brother's gone! You've got to help me find him, everyone! You've got to help me now!'

And everyone realised immediately what a disaster it was. The human child, who they'd all been so excited about meeting, was missing.

'We must locate him,' ordered Queen Alisha, joining Nita up on the stage, and wearing her sternest, most determined expression. 'You've had your fun, everyone. Now search my palace, from top to bottom, and find him!'

So every single one of the amadans stopped what they were doing and began to look for the lost little human: under the tables, up in the tower, down in the cellar, out in the yard – in fact, anywhere and everywhere they could think of. The floodlights were thrown on, inside the castle and out, the sirens were sounded, and every nook and cranny was investigated. But, try as they might, no one could find a single sign of him. Not anywhere.

But then Haranga, scouring the yard for clues, went to look through the window into the hall, in case by any chance Partho had found his way back on to the dance floor. And it was then that he saw the giant footprints.

'Eek!' he cried in an anguished voice, recognising them immediately. (Well, not quite immediately. First he thought they were his own, but when he put his foot in one to check, he realised it was bigger. Much bigger.) 'It must be Sonya!'

'Who? Where?' asked Nita, running over.

'Sonya...' said Haranga, pointing at the footprint and turning pale. 'My big sister. She must have come to find me.'

'Your big sister!' said Nita, horrified at the very thought. 'You never told us you had a sister!'

'Do you mean to say there are others like you?' cried the Queen, who'd heard Haranga's strangled eek and rushed over to see what he'd found. 'I mean, one dumb monster's bad enough...'

'Don't tell me she's taken my Partho?' whispered Nita.

'I'm sure she won't have hurt him,' Haranga responded, trying to put himself in Sonya's position. Trying to think as she would have thought. 'She's a tough cookie, my sister – you have to be where we come from – but she's never cruel, not unless she really has to be. But I think she might have found him,' he said. For even to a monster of little brain, like Haranga, it seemed fairly obvious that the sudden appearance of Sonya and the mysterious disappearance of little Partho, at the same time, might well go hand-in-hand. 'And I'm afraid she might have taken him away.'

'But why?' Nita gasped. 'If you say she's not cruel, then why would she do such a thing?'

'Maybe because she's lonely. I went off and abandoned her, you see,' Haranga confessed. 'We lived together for thousands of years but I got fed up with her bossing me about, so I woke up one morning, early, and decided to wander off on my own. I walked and I walked and, when it came to the point where I probably should have turned back, I didn't. I just carried on walking. Through the snow, over the mountains, through the forest, over the next mountains, until…'

'Until you came to the caves above NetherEdge?' suggested the Queen.

'Exactly,' said Haranga. 'And there I set up shop.'

'Free from the bossiness of a big sister,' said Nita. 'Free to be as nasty as you liked. Free to boss everyone else about, for a change.'

'Exactly.'

'But what you didn't know was that your big sister wouldn't let you go... What you didn't know was that she'd wake up and start to follow you...'

'Exactly,' said Haranga. 'I knew she wouldn't be happy that I'd gone off without her, but I didn't for one minute think she'd follow me all the way to NetherEdge.'

'Well, the good thing about snow, if you're trying to follow someone,' said Nita, thinking logically as ever, despite the desperate situation in which she found herself, 'is that it makes it very easy to track them. Especially someone as big as you.'

'So she followed you to NetherEdge,' added the Queen, nodding. 'And eventually to my palace. And my party.'

'Yes, I suppose so,' said Haranga, thinking about his poor sister's journey. 'It must have been so hard for her. And so cold...'

'So she lost her little brother,' declared Nita, putting the whole thing together, 'and she decided to take mine, instead! Because when she eventually found you, when she saw you through this window, there you were, all pretty-pretty dancing…'

'With me,' said Alisha.

'Yes, Ma'am' said Nita, before turning back to Haranga. 'She knew she'd never win you back,' she told him, 'so she made up her mind to take an easier catch instead. My Partho!'

'I'm afraid so.' Haranga nodded. 'But I'm sure she won't have meant him any harm. She's just a big soppy sister.'

'No harm!' cried a furious Nita. 'I don't want your sister anywhere near my little brother! We'd better get him back, safe and sound, or you'll be sorry, Haranga!'

'Yes,' said the down-in-the-mouth monster. 'We will. I promise.'

'It's your fault, Haranga!' cried Nita, suddenly more angry than she'd ever been in her whole entire life. 'If you hadn't run off and abandoned her, she'd never have stolen him!'

'I know. I'm sorry.'

'But I'll get him back,' Nita vowed. 'Because he's not hers, he's mine! And just like that sister of yours, Haranga, I shall track little Partho down, even if I have to go to the very ends of the earth to find him. And when I meet up with your Sonya, she'd better watch out!'

'Yes,' said Haranga. 'Of course.'

'And you're coming with me!' she ordered.

'Yes,' said Haranga. 'Of course.'

And he racked his brains to think where Sonya might have taken the little boy, and what she might have done with him and how on earth they were going to get him back.

25
ONWARDS AND UPWARDS

Poor Partho's feet were sore from the dust and the gravel, the barley and the straw, but he carried on, regardless. Haranga was good. He was a friend of Nita and Jimmy's. Little Partho had no reason to distrust him, and every reason to be excited at the idea of being taken somewhere special by him.

When they'd gone far enough from the Queen's palace for Sonya to feel safe, she found a barn, well away from any habitation, where they could rest up for the night. Realising by now that the little boy must have mistaken her for her brother, Sonya made sure he didn't get a good look at her.

'Lie down and sleep, little fellow,' she muttered. 'Tomorrow I shall take you to the special place.'

'Will it be fun?' asked Partho. 'Will I like it there?'

'Mmmm,' said Sonya, and Partho, worn out from all the singing and dancing, laughing and playing, and even more exhausted from all that never-ending walking, lay down in the hay and slept soundly.

Haranga's big sister stayed awake all night, watching over him as he slept, and keeping an eye out for anyone who might discover them, especially her brother and the amadans.

No one came and all was quiet, but everything changed as soon as Partho woke. 'Who are you?' he cried, in a frightened voice. 'Where are we going?' For, in the clear light of morning, it was perfectly obvious to him that although the creature he was with bore a striking similarity to his friend, Haranga, it was, most definitely, NOT Haranga.

'I am Sonya, Haranga's sister,' she told him. 'There is nothing to fear.'

'He never mentioned you,' said the little boy, frowning. 'Where are you taking me?'

'To a special place, remember,' said the monster. 'Jump up now, for we must be on our way.'

And so, revived by a good night's rest, they were off again. Partho wasn't at all happy, though, for he couldn't understand why this Sonya had pretended to be her brother. And he couldn't understand why she should be leading him away from Nita and the amadans. But he knew that for now, anyway, he had no choice but to go with her. The only alternative was to try and escape, but this was a strange land to him, and he had no idea how to find his way back to the palace.

Sonya kept to the darkest lanes and hedges, determined to avoid discovery, for she knew that what she had done would have repercussions. She knew, beyond any shadow of a doubt, that word would have gone out to every inhabitant of this strange country that a human child had gone missing, and that it was the absolute duty of each and every one of them to watch out for him, to rescue him from wherever he'd found himself, or from whatever or whomsoever had taken him, and to return him to the Queen as soon as possible.

But Sonya felt no guilt, for she had rescued little Partho from the amadans, and now she had her very own little human and, oh, how happy she was! She would never be lonely again. She would give him all the love and attention that she never had from her absent parents. All the love and attention that she'd tried to give to Haranga, once her mother and father had disappeared for ever into the frozen snow. (Only she didn't really know how to look after a helpless big lump at the time, as she was only young herself. Not only that, she was inconsolable with grief, as you would be if your parents had just disappeared off the face of the planet without so much as a by-your-leave.)

Eventually, Sonya began to lead Partho upwards, towards the mountains, towards the start of the long trek home. But as soon as she started to go uphill, she felt a deep ache in her legs. An ache that quickly developed, with every step, into a searing pain.

Sonya was tired, so tired. She had walked so far, for so long, to find her long-lost brother, and on such an empty stomach, too, after the failed Hundred Year Hunt. Through the snow, mile upon mile, over the mountains and down the other side, over the next lot of mountains and down the other side, she had gone, until she felt she could never climb another hill again. Not now, anyway. Not without a long, long rest, and there was no time for any more rest. The amadans were on her trail. They were coming after her, to take back from her the lovely little human she had rescued.

And she wasn't sure young Partho had the energy to climb, either. He looked so tired, the poor little mite. No, Sonya realised, there was no way she or the tiny human were likely to get all the way home. No, this time, her hideout would have to be somewhere different. Somewhere nearer.

She scanned the landscape all around, looking for somewhere safe to hide, and then she remembered. Haranga's cave! The one she had come across earlier. The one that was all collapsed inside. Yes, that was the place to go.

'Come on, little one,' she said in her kindest voice. 'It's not far.'

But when she turned around, to encourage the boy to keep up, he was nowhere to be seen. 'Partho! Where are you, Partho!' she cried.

There was no response.

She ran back to the bend in the path, and there, far below and running away at top speed, was the tiny human.

'Stop! Stop!' she cried. And she hared down the hill after him, as fast as her tired and weary legs would carry her.

Partho was determined to escape, though. He'd had enough of being hoodwinked, enough of trekking up mountains with a monster he'd never met before. Even if he didn't know how to find his way back to Jimmy, Nita and the amadans, he'd decided to make a break for it.

But he'd forgotten about the mighty river that they'd crossed only a few minutes before. The mighty fast-flowing river, where Sonya had had to pick him up and raise him high on her shoulders, in order to carry him across.

He came to the bank and ran up and down, desperately looking for a safe place. There wasn't one, and when he turned back he saw Sonya, rushing down the hill towards him.

He couldn't let her catch him again! He couldn't and he wouldn't, so he ran straight into the river, hoping his speed would carry him through. But the water was shockingly cold. Partho gasped, trying to force his way through the surging current, but he was no more than halfway across when he slipped on a slimy underwater rock and the power of the freezing river knocked him off his feet.

'Help!' he yelled, as he fell headlong into, and then under, the raging water. He surfaced only to find that he was being carried downstream at high speed, with no possible way of slowing himself down. And what he didn't know, and it wouldn't have done him any good even if he had, was that the relentless power of the water was drawing him closer and closer to the edge of a massive and terrifying waterfall.

And that would have been that. End of story for the plucky little fellow. (For he was either going to drown in the deep and swirling pool at the bottom of the mighty drop, or split his head apart on the rocks on the way down, or both.) Closer and closer to the edge went little Partho, with absolutely no chance of preventing himself from careering downwards to oblivion, when suddenly, at the very last minute, he felt himself being pulled up and out and free of the river.

It was Sonya. She had waded into the raging water and rescued him!

'I'm sorry! I'm sorry, little fellow,' she said, laying him on the grass and pumping the water out of him. 'Are you all right?'

Partho sploshed and splurted, but eventually he came round. 'Yes,' he said, grudgingly. 'Yes, I think so.'

'You didn't need to run away,' Sonya told him. 'I'm only trying to take care of you.' And she leaned out to caress his face.

'I don't need taking care of!' cried Partho, his teeth chattering. 'I just want to go home.'

For even though the shivering boy was grateful to the mighty monster for saving him from the freezing water, he was furious too, for he knew that it had only happened because she'd kidnapped him.

'You're half frozen, you poor thing!' cried Sonya, who was beginning to regret what she'd done. 'I need to get you out of this biting wind. Here, let me carry you.'

The power to resist had gone out of Partho, and she lifted him up, cradling him in her arms and carried him up to Haranga's lair, where she made him as comfortable as possible amid the debris of fallen rocks at the back of the cave.

'Here, let me lie next to you. That'll warm you up,' she said, kissing his sweet little, frozen little face. And Partho, who was too shocked and exhausted to object, soon found himself snuggling into her warmth, and sleeping soundly.

26
SHOWDOWN

'Tracks!' cried Haranga, pointing at the ground.

Jimmy and Nita came running to see, and he was right.

'It must be Sonya,' cried Nita, utterly sickened at the thought of what had become of her poor little, lost little brother.

They rushed off to find Queen Alisha and to tell her what they'd found. 'You must follow the tracks and find out what's become of him,' she agreed. 'But be careful, my friends. Be very careful!'

'Sonya won't have harmed him,' said Haranga, trying to reassure Nita and Jimmy as they went. 'I'm sure she won't.'

But Nita was frantic. 'Not harmed him!' she

yelled. 'Your whacking great lump of a sister steals away my sweet little brother and you say she hasn't harmed him! Are you out of your tiny mind?'

'He'll be fine,' muttered Haranga. 'It's only because she's lonely.'

'He will not be fine!' Nita screeched back at him. 'Not unless we find him, and find him soon! And if you can't keep that sister of yours under some sort of control, you great clumsy muddlehead, then the least you can do is lead me to her!'

Haranga didn't much like being called a great clumsy muddlehead, but he understood how desperate poor Nita must feel, so he didn't respond. He knew there was nothing more he could do, anyway, not till they'd tracked Sonya down. So off they went, all three of them, determined to find little Partho and rescue him from his fate.

Every now and again they'd lose the way, for the tracks weren't easy to follow without snow. But each time, if they fanned out and threw the search a bit wider, looking for soft ground or indentations in the grass, they managed to pick up at least one more print. And once they'd got Haranga to stand in it, to make sure it was Sonya's and not his, they could usually tell, by the direction it seemed to be pointing, where to look out for the next one.

And so, by a mixture of detection, deduction and luck, they arrived at the barn.

'He's been here! I know he has!' cried Nita, finding a Partho-sized indentation in the hay.

The three of them decided to rest up for the night, pleased with their progress, and in the morning they followed on, like a trio of supersleuth bloodhounds, until they came to the foothills of the Great Mountain.

'Yes, it's just as I thought,' said Haranga, looking in the direction of his previous home. 'She'll have taken him up there. Up to the caves.'

'Oh no!' Jimmy had a sinking feeling, remembering all that had happened before. 'Not again!'

But there was no choice. Despite the memory of the awful events that had occurred the last time they were all there, up at the cave (when it was nearly curtains for both Jimmy and Haranga), on they walked, upwards, ever upwards.

'Poor Partho,' said Jimmy, panting for breath. 'He'll be so tired.'

'All I want,' said Nita, striding on ahead, 'is to see him alive.'

'Of course he's alive,' said Haranga, following close behind. 'Sonya might have wanted to steal him away, to ease her loneliness, but I'm sure she wouldn't hurt him. It's just not in her nature to do such a thing. The only time she'd ever hurt anyone is if she's being attacked. Or if she's hungry, and she needs to eat.'

One look at Nita's face told him that this was not the best thing to say.

Haranga called out then, in his loudest, deepest, most mournful voice. 'Sonya! Are you up there, Sonya?'

But there was no answer. His sister, in the depths of the cave, could hear him by now, though, for they were really rather close, and the sound of her lost brother's voice, crying out to her, cut her to the heart. But there was no way she was going to respond. For she had no doubt that despite all the many, many miles she'd travelled to find Haranga, that his reason for coming back up the mountain to find her wasn't in order to tell her how much he loved her and how sorry he was that he'd run away.

Oh no, he'd come to help those nasty little goblin creatures she'd seen through the window steal away her little one – the beautiful human child that she'd always desired! And she wasn't going to let him. In fact, she wasn't going to let him anywhere near!

Sonya felt safe, deep in the heart of the cave. She knew that something had once happened there to her great lump of a brother, for she had smelled his fear when she'd been there before, and she could still smell it, all around her.

She knew, too, that the other puny trackers would be too scared to come in and confront someone so much bigger and stronger than themselves. But she still didn't want to answer. All she wanted was for them to go away and leave her with her precious little, cosy little, sweet little human.

'Partho!' cried Nita, as they arrived at the entrance. 'Are you in there, Partho?'

Her little brother stirred from his sleep. Nita! It was Nita, his lovely sister, come to rescue him. He tried to sit up, but something was holding him down. And when he tried to cry out he found that there was a great hairy arm over his mouth, preventing him from even speaking.

But Sonya was wrong about Haranga. Yes, he was nervous about re-entering the cave after the incredibly close shave he'd had the last time he'd been in there, but his determination to rescue little Partho overrode his fears.

'I'm going in to find him!' the monster declared, storming forward. 'I'm going to march straight in there and demand him back!'

'No!' yelled Nita, who was a great believer in looking before you leap. 'Wait!'

'Don't worry,' cried the monster, who wasn't. 'I'll be fine.'

He marched straight into the cave and, without waiting for his eyes to adjust to the darkness (like you're supposed to in a dark place), headed directly for the back, where he knew he was likely to find Sonya and little Partho.

Unfortunately, though, Haranga forgot about the freezehole – the mighty great chasm in the dead centre of the cave where he used to store his food or his prisoners. He also forgot, too, that the floor of the cave was littered with mighty fallen rocks. So yes – you guessed it – he tripped on a rock, went flying forward and fell straight down the freezehole. Crash, bang, wallop.

'Haranga!' cried Sonya, who'd seen it all happening (her eyes, of course, were much better adjusted to the dark as she'd been in there for ages). And she let go of Partho and ran forward.

At which point, Nita took the opportunity to dash in, and past her. She knelt down on her hands and knees next to her little brother, and kissed him.

'Nita!' the seven-year-old cried.

'Partho!'

'I want to go home,' he moaned, in a faint little-boy-lost sort of voice.

But suddenly, 'Oh no, you don't!' hissed Sonya, who'd seen someone flash past her. And she turned away from the freezehole and ran back to grab her precious little human from what she thought, out of the corner of her eye, must be an amadan, come to steal him away.

'Don't you dare TOUCH him!' roared Nita.

'Keep your thieving hands away,' yelled Sonya, pushing her aside and taking hold of him. 'He's my coochy-coochy boy, and he's staying with me!'

'You keep YOUR thieving hands away!' screamed Nita, flailing at her. 'He's MY BROTHER!'

And there was a stunned silence. 'Your brother?' said Sonya, amazed.

But then, 'STOP GRABBING AT ME!' cried Partho, sitting up. 'Why does everyone have to keep pulling and tugging me all the time? Why does everyone keep trying to kiss me? Just leave me alone, will you?'

And he jumped to his feet and stomped off, out of the cave, leaving the other two to sort it out between them.

'Is he really your brother?' whispered Sonya. 'Your flesh-and-blood brother?'

'Of course he is,' said Nita. 'Just like Haranga is yours.'

And in that moment, Sonya's ties with the human child evaporated and all the female monster wanted was to be back with the last remaining member of her family. Her very own big little brother, who she'd spent all those many many hundreds of years with, in their cosy cave high in the mountains.

And, as if on cue, a cry arose from the bottom of the freezehole. 'Sonya!' bellowed Haranga. 'Help me!'

Sonya returned then, to the edge of the drop, looked down at her long-lost brother, and a wave of affection broke over her. She reached her arm down, Haranga stretched his up, but, despite the fact that they were both bigger than any other living creature, they couldn't reach each other.

'Hang on a minute,' said Sonya. 'I'll just chuck

some rocks down for you to climb up on.'

And she grabbed a load of boulders and flung them down into the hole.

'OK, see if you can reach now!' she yelled, but there was no response.

'You've brained him, you great bumbling nitwit!' cried Nita, who'd come over to see what was going on. 'You must be as dim as your brother!'

And sure enough, when they looked down, they could just about make out Haranga, lying on the ground, moaning, with a massive pile of rocks on his belly.

'Duhhhh,' he said, pushing them off, for luckily, he was big enough and squishy enough to withstand such an onslaught without more than a few cuts and bruises. 'What did you do that for, you clumsy oaf?'

'Serves you right for going off without me, fatso,' said Sonya, who wasn't too good at apologies. Not when she'd just been insulted, not just once but twice.

'Oh, stop arguing,' said Nita. 'Let's just get him out of there.'

So clever-clogs Nita gave out the instructions, and then Sonya lay face-down on the ground and dangled her arm over the edge of the drop, while

Haranga piled all the rocks up, balanced on the top – wibbly, wobbly – and stretched out his arm, as high as it would go, wriggling his fingers around in the hope that his dearly beloved sister might be just about able to reach them.

And she could! For Sonya, at full stretch, grabbed hold of his wrist, and with Jimmy pulling on Sonya's other arm, Nita pulling on his, and Partho pulling on Nita's, they all hauled at the same time. ('One, two, three, TUG!' yelled Nita.) And up came the mightily heavy Haranga, up and out of the hole.

'Haranga!' Sonya squeaked, as he slithered out to safety. 'You look so – messy!'

And he did. So wonderfully, wonderfully mucky, after trekking through the rain and the mud, after splashing about in the muck and bones at the bottom of the freezehole, after being bashed on the bonce by all the rocks his kind and loving sister had toppled down on top of him.

Yes, he looked so much better to her than the pretty-pretty dancer he'd been, waltzing with the Queen, when she'd rediscovered him after her long and arduous trek. So much more like the clumsy great carbuncle that she'd always cared for and loved.

'Can we go home now, Haranga?' Sonya pleaded, echoing the words of little Partho.

And her big little brother smiled. 'Maybe,' he said, nodding. 'But not all the way over the mountains to where we used to live. Why don't we set up home here? That way I can still live the wild and woolly outdoor life with you, but be close to my new friends, too.'

For Haranga knew what he wanted, at last. He'd burned out all his anger, at last. All his frustration at always being bossed about by his big sister, all the loneliness of living in a cave, miles from anywhere.

He'd thought, once he'd managed to escape Sonya's clutches, that what he needed was power and domination, but discovered, through the help of Jimmy, Nita and the amadans, that all he wanted, really, was to be liked and be loved, like anyone else.

So Nita agreed that if Sonya agreed to live with Haranga in the cave, and stopped trying to kidnap little Partho, she'd forgive her for kidnapping her little brother. And Sonya, who by now wanted nothing more than to play happy families with her very own big little brother again, agreed. (Even if he wasn't quite as wild and woolly as he used to be, and even if he wasn't as likely to let her get away with bossing him about all the time like he used to, now that he'd broken free from her influence.)

Then the others went back, while Haranga and Sonya did what they could to rebuild the cave. It took many days of hard slog, pushing aside the rocks that had fallen down at the entrance, lifting great pillars of stone from the floor to prop up the roof inside, clearing out the debris from when the walls had fallen in. Not forgetting asking the permission of the thousand and eight bats who still lived there whether it would be all right to come and join them, and reassuring them that this time their new neighbours would be well-behaved, friendly and would, in fact, spend most of their time sleeping.

And eventually, with a load of help from the amadans, like Fleur, Jola, Dunk and the others, who came up to help (they didn't dare go inside, not after what had happened last time, but they helped clear away some of the debris so it didn't just all pile up at the entrance to the cave) it became a suitable home for a monster and his sister.

Once everyone was convinced that the roof was

safe and there wasn't any danger of the whole thing collapsing again, they decided to be brave enough to venture inside. And they had a very jolly cave-warming party, to which everyone was invited, including Jimmy, Nita, Grandad and Partho (who'd already been back home by now, where nobody'd even missed them, as they'd only been away about ten minutes, human time), as well as the whole cast of amadans: Bun, Dunk, Queen Alisha and everyone else who'd got to know Haranga in the time he'd spent with them.

And then, once Sonya and Haranga's new home was well and truly warmed and they'd gone off to curl up together at the back of the cave for an early hundred-year sleep, which they'd well and truly earned after all that effort and excitement, it was time for everyone else to get back to business...

Jimmy and Nita to getting on with their lives, as they were before they'd met the amadans (though they rather hoped it wasn't the last time they'd see them);

Partho to perfecting his wheelies and zoomers on his shiny aluminium top-of-the-range feather-weight mountain bike, complete with twenty-four speed fire-trigger gears, state-of-the-art fully active suspension, stop-dead shimano brakes, go-faster helmet (and a brand-new no-way-you're-getting-through-this chain, for locking the whole thing up at night, just in case);

Jimmy's dad to getting back to the Great Irish Novel (and I'm sure you'll be pleased to hear that he'd been to see his dentist, who'd told him to cut down on the chocolate biscuits);

Jimmy's grandad to going back to the quiet life of eating a big bowl of porridge for breakfast, dozing in his armchair, and telling tales about the good old days to anyone and everyone who'd listen – activities much better suited to a man of a thousand and six (or whatever);

Steady George and Black-Eyed Pete to being decent law-abiding citizens, for as long as they could manage it, which probably wasn't likely to be very long, but you never know;

Dizzy Belle to running her café without interference or food-poisoning;

Barry Frizzle to putting the bad old days of being a smirky lurky teenage sneakthief behind him and going off to college to train to be a television engineer;

Bun to carrying on as Official Gatekeeper of the SuperHighway, keeping control of all the comings-and-goings of the crimestopper squad – for their work wasn't over yet, not by a long chalk (the effectiveness of the Stroke, by the way, seemed to be slowly returning, now that Haranga had settled down);

...and Queen Alisha to continue ruling the ever-alert amadans, kindly, fiercely, wisely and well.

OTHER RED APPLES TO GET
YOUR TEETH INTO . . .

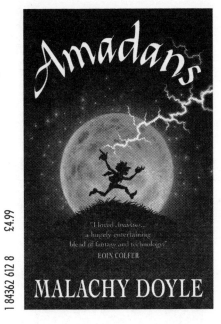

1 84362 612 8   £4.99

MALACHY DOYLE

"I've had enough of these Amadans, trying to scare everyone,' said Jimmy. 'I think it's about time we found out who they are and what they're up to.'

Enter the fantastical world of the Amadans in this enthralling read.

"I loved Amadans…a hugely entertaining blend of fantasy and technology."
EOIN COLFER

FIONA DUNBAR

Imagine a magical recipe to make all your dreams come true!

Lulu Baker's dad has a new love, Varaminta le Bone. She's a sizzling sensation...and pure poison. How can Lulu make her dad see Varaminta for who she really is?

A mysterious recipe book and some very unusual ingredients just might do the trick...

£4.99

1 84121 810 3

when mum threw out the telly

e.f. smith
A SMARTIES AWARD WINNING AUTHOR

EMILY SMITH

Jeff really liked television. Cartoons were more
interesting than life. Sit-coms were funnier than life.
And in life you never got to watch someone trying
to ride a bike over an open sewer. Sometimes at night
Jeff even dreamed television. Mum complained, but
it didn't make any difference. Jeff didn't take any
notice of her, which was a mistake.

A very funny and thought-provoking book from
Emily Smith, winner of two Smarties Prizes.

£4.99

1 84362 134 7

CHRIS D'LACEY

When David Rain is set an essay on dragons,
there's only one thing he knows for sure – he
wants to win the prize of a research trip to the
Arctic. As David begins to dig deeper into the
past, he finds himself drawn down a path from
which there is not going back... to the very heart
of the legend of dragons, and the mysterious,
ancient secret of the icefire.

Chris d'Lacey's book, *Fly Cherokee, Fly,* was highly
commended for the Carnegie Medal.

£4.99

1 84362 187 8

ANDREW MATTHEWS

Dido Nesbit is no ordinary girl – she's a Light
Witch. But being a modern-day witch isn't easy –
not when you've got to juggle magic with
schoolwork, friends and all the usual problems a
girl has to deal with.

There are another two titles in *The Light Witch*
trilogy to read!

MORE ORCHARD RED APPLES

❏ *Amadans*	Malachy Doyle	1 84362 612 8
❏ *Utterly Me, Clarice Bean*	Lauren Child	1 84362 304 8
❏ *Clarice Bean Spells Trouble*	Lauren Child	1 84362 858 9
❏ *The Fire Within*	Chris d'Lacey	1 84121 533 3
❏ *Icefire*	Chris d'Lacey	1 84362 134 7
❏ *Shrinking Ralph Perfect*	Chris d'Lacey	1 84362 660 8
❏ *Cupid Cakes*	Fiona Dunbar	1 84362 688 8
❏ *The Truth Cookie*	Fiona Dunbar	1 84362 549 0
❏ *Do Not Read This Book*	Pat Moon	1 84121 435 3
❏ *Tower-block Pony*	Alison Prince	1 84362 648 9
❏ *The Secret Life of Jamie B.* *Superspy*	Ceri Worman	1 84362 389 7

All priced at £4.99

Orchard Red Apples are available from all good bookshops,
or can be ordered direct from the publisher:
Orchard Books, PO BOX 29, Douglas IM99 1BQ
Credit card orders please telephone 01624 836000
or fax 01624 837033
or visit our Internet site: www.wattspub.co.uk
or e-mail: bookshop@enterprise.net for details.

To order please quote title, author and ISBN
and your full name and address.
Cheques and postal orders should be made payable to 'Bookpost plc.'
Postage and packing is FREE within the UK
(overseas customers should add £1.00 per book)

Prices and availability are subject to change.